FORGETLESS

Shadowline™

image

ShadowlineOnline.com

FORGETLESS

SECOND PRINTING, **MAY 2012**

ISBN: 978-1-60706-460-2

DISCOVER EVERYTHING NOW!

tweetie

TOP TWEETIES See all

NICK SPENCER

To Julie, Casey, Seb, Aileen, and Kendall... and all the friends back home I never forget.

Posted 2 mins ago

MARLEY ZARCONE

To my husband, my family and my friends. Also to Nick for inviting me to participate in this wonderful book!

Posted 10 mins ago

SCOTT FORBES

To my dad, mom, brothers, and friends - thanks for supporting me!

Posted 7 mins ago

JORGE COELHO

For all that's real and good, thanks Luciano, Belmira, Sónia and Carla! You are the best.

Posted 5 mins ago

TIM DANIEL

Elle, Erin, Jim, Kris, Nick, thanks for allowing me to fulfill my dream!

Posted 3 days ago

FORGETLESS

LIVE TO SEE LAST CALL

AUTHOR NICK SPENCER

COVER W. SCOTT FORBES

ARTISTS W. SCOTT FORBES
MARLEY ZARCONE
JORGE COELHO

COLORS W. SCOTT FORBES
ERIC SKILLMAN
MARLEY ZARCONE

LETTERS JOHNNY LOWE

EDITOR JADE DODGE

PUBLISHER JIM VALENTINO

DESIGN TIM DANIEL

COMMUNICATIONS MARC LOMBARDI

image comics, inc.//www.imagecomics.com

Robert Kirkman - chief operating officer
Erik Larsen - chief financial officer
Todd McFarlane - president
Marc Silvestri - chief executive officer
Jim Valentino - vice-president
Eric Stephenson - publisher

Todd Martinez - sales & licensing coordinator
Jennifer de Guzman - pr & marketing director
Branwyn Bigglestone - accounts manager
Emily Miller - administrative assistant
Jamie Parreno - marketing assistant
Sarah deLaine - events coordinator
Kevin Yuen - digital rights coordinator

Tyler Shainline - production manager
Drew Gill - art director
Jonathan Chan - senior production artist
Monica Garcia - production artist
Vincent Kukua - production artist
Jana Cook - production artist

INTRO SPENCER'S LAST CALL

People love New York. It's true. There are even t-shirts available that proclaim that very statement, complete with a big red heart to symbolize all that juicy love. It's a city of dreams, of hustlers and playboys, chorus girls and rockers, artists and writers, all of whom are probably waiting tables as you read this. If you can make it there, you can make it anywhere, according to Frank. Sinatra, that is, but you knew that. It's a city where you can famously get anything you want at any hour of the day. You can order Chinese, a new sofa, and a bag of marijuana, and have them all delivered to your doorstep at 3 A.M. by a bike messenger who's studying Romance Languages at NYU. New York City. There's nothing you can't do, according to Alicia. Keys, that is, but you knew that.

People hate New York. It's true. There are even t-shirts available that proclaim that. Well, actually, they read "Yankees Suck", but that's pretty much the same thing. It's an equivalent, The Bronx Bombers being such a symbol for the city. New York is a dirty, dense, over-crowded urban tangle of concrete and garbage piled in endless mounds on every street. The summers are thick with sticky humidity; the winters clogged with dirty, befouled icy slush; the air throughout the canyons reeking of urine regardless of season. There is never a moment's peace in New York City, as the streets and sidewalks remain crowded with cabs and delivery men, dropping off furniture and Chinese food at all hours of the day. Rents are impossibly high, only the trust-fund generation can live comfortably, and all the artists and writers, chorus girls and rockers, are forced to wait tables and live in studios in Queens with three roommates apiece. Most people are so rent-poor they spend their time feeling beat down, trapped, and helpless.

New York City is complicated. People's feelings toward New York often are informed by the fantasy of NYC, the televised image of endless flickering re-runs of Seinfeld and Law & Order, Sex & The City and Friends. They feel the pulse of the city in the endless looping mixtape of indigenous music; the wail of a Charlie Parker alto solo that gives way to the simmering strum of Bob Dylan that leads into the dissonant drone of the Velvet Underground that begets the three-chord-glue-sniffing blast of The Ramones that births the post-Modern nostalgic ennui of The Strokes. New York exists in all five senses, for better or worse. You can taste it, even. There is a taste in the winter in Mid-Town that is unmistakable, almost disgusting, yet oddly comforting, because despite the funk of it, it's New York. It's home.

Darla Danberry loves New York. Darla Danberry is a teenage girl from South Jersey who wears a garish red faux-fur Russian ushanka and white leather 8-hole Doc Marten boots. She designs clothes, has a gay male BFF named David who spins, records that is. He DJs in playgrounds because he's a teenager, too. They both have a friend named Leigh who, well, doesn't say much of anything. She's just there with them, an anchor of chill to keep the group together. They're childhood friends who've grown up together in the 'burbs of the Big Apple, and have all internalized the common malady of kids raised in Jersey, that of inbred inferiority combined with grandiose ambitions. They're wannabes. They wannabe free. They wannabe famous. They wannabe older so they can get into the big night clubs, run their own parties, live the televised fantasy of New York. They've drunk the fairy-tale Kool-Aid and on the side of the bottle are the letters N-Y-C.

Sara Schmidt hates New York. Sara Schmidt is a college-aged quote-unquote model living in downtown Manhattan who doesn't seem to like much of anything, except a particularly bad late-night talk show host - oh, and killing people. For money. That's what she really does for a living. She's a model ostensibly only because she's signed to one of the many random model agencies that populate New York; in actuality she's been hired by a shadow agency to be a covert assassin. Sara is essentially heartless; taking the cool-as-ice aloofness of your average urban hipster to a ruthless extreme. She won't just make fun of the clothes you wear or the music you listen to, she'll stab you sixty times with a knife. Without blinking. She's a disease. She infects her roommate Sonia, also a model. They're wannabes, too. They wannabe on the covers of Vogue, supposedly. Really, it seems, they just wannabe making money while staving off boredom.

Then there is Derrick, a college-aged prankster, aimless and shuffling, who loves New York so much he copulates with it, literally. He has sex with inanimate objects - buildings, espresso machines, mops - and films it, posts it online. He is an internet star, his videos garnering hundreds of thousands of hits a day. In the city built by men such as Carnegie, Morgan, and Rockefeller, a city that celebrates the ideals of self-actualization, therein enter Derrick, the self-made celebrity, thrusting away in a crack in the Empire State Building. Most people feel screwed by the Big City; Derrick returns the favor.

This is the story of Forgetless. This is the bizarre, complicated, hilariously sick mess that Nick Spencer has created. It is a world overstuffed with absurdity, yet one that flirts with fairy-tale. It's that uncomfortable artistic contradiction rearing around again; this is truth dressed in the most unbelievably ridiculous fiction. Writer Nick Spencer weaves these contradictory tales with effortless skill, balancing the muck of cynicism against the gleaming light of optimism, and shows how this duality informs every moment of life in the urban jungle of New York. These very real people ground all the surreality. The parts of the story that are sick and depraved ring even more frightening, while those moments that show heart shine with true hopefulness. That he gives all these characters, to varying degrees, some form of "happy ending", is a true testament to his deftness.

Mr. Spencer doesn't work alone, and a crime of this magnitude requires accomplices of the highest order. Scott Forbes brings a clean quality to his pages, with a thin line weight and shiny surface that give Sara and Sonia that gaunt under-fed model look. He provides a world where backgrounds are sparse color fields blurred around the edge, as if large-scale Rothko's have been hung to form stage flats for sets. This allows the bold expressiveness of his characters to pop even more.

Jorge Coelho's work is far more detailed and carries with it the essence of underground comics in that it provides a cartoony veneer to very realistic settings. He draws the majority of issue #4, which centers on the story of a certain talk-show host as he tells tale of his sexual activities involving online personal ads and a Koala suit. (Yeah, it's that kind of story.) His style fits this perfectly; certain panels having a frenzied and crowded-to-bursting quality reminiscent of mid-60's MAD Magazine, which accentuates the deviant tone of this chapter.

Then enters the incomparable Marley Zarcone, whose storytelling and characterization all crackle with living energy. Zarcone's real success is Darla Danberry. Darla is the engine that moves this entire series; she is a stand-out figure whose personality looms large on the city landscape, and Zarcone fills her with blood and guts, humanity and verve, right down to the David Letterman-style gap between her two front teeth. Spencer gives some of the funniest and sharpest lines to Darla and Zarcone sets about to match the pose, posture, and facial expression perfectly to drive each witticism, each barb, each deft turn of phrase deep into the skin. by story's end, Darla positively lives and breathes as surely as a person standing next to you on the subway. I can't imagine reading too many more characters stronger than she in comics this year. Darla Danberry is my new hero, and Zarcone and Spencer stand as the hero-makers.

Forgetless is a New York story, through and through. It vibrates with the very rhythms that propel that city and its populace every single wonderfully lousy, god-forsaken day. It recognizes the heartbreak of New York, laments that which is seemingly missing, like an amputee forlorn over a lost limb. Yet it celebrates the ability for New York to provide redemption, hope, and even miracles at any given moment. Serendipity isn't just a candy store, it's a way of life. In a City of hope. In a City where anything is possible. It's 3 A.M. Your dream is here.

Ramon Gamboa
August, 2010

Ramon Gamboa is the creator of the daily comic strip, LBD. Whenever possible, he lives in New York City, alone.

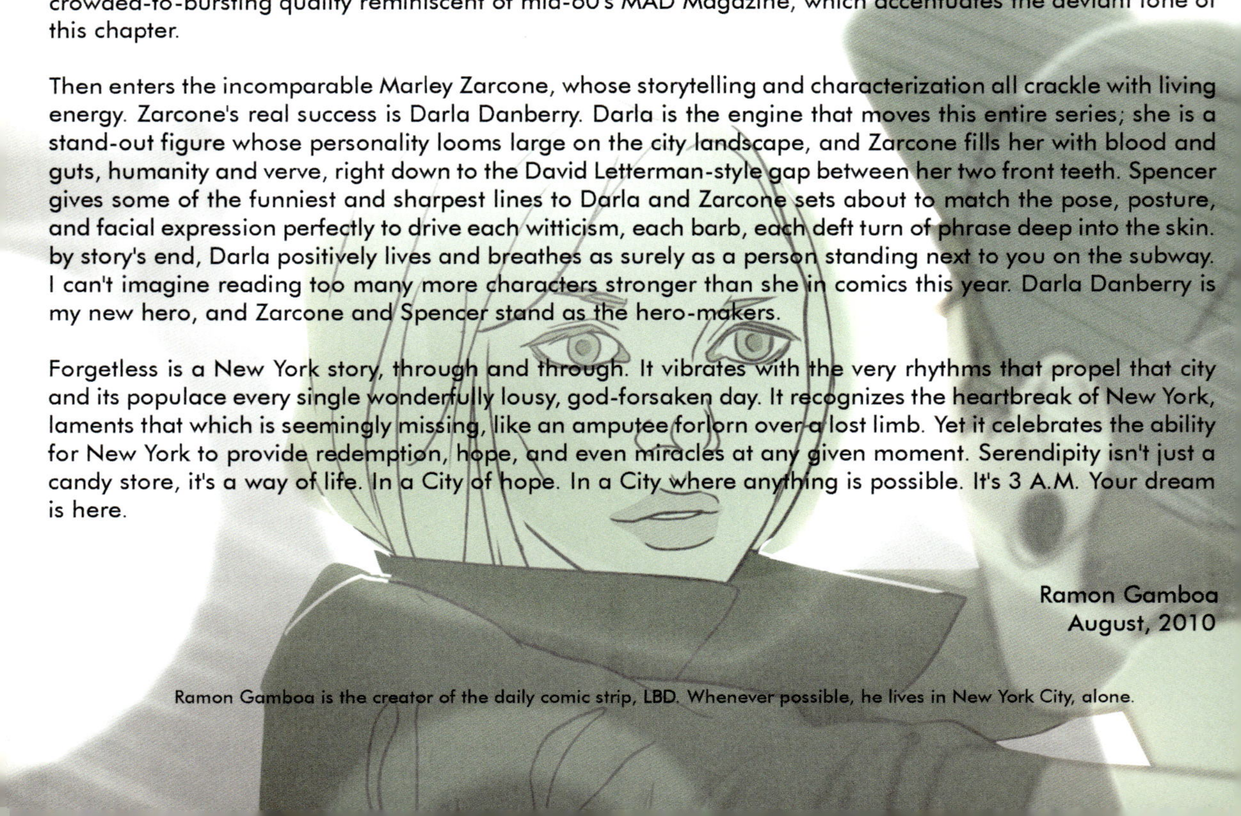

PART 1

LIVE TO SEE LAST CALL

W. SCOTT FORBES
ART & COLORS

JORGE COELHO
ART

COLORS
ERIC SKILLMAN

LETTERS
JOHNNY LOWE

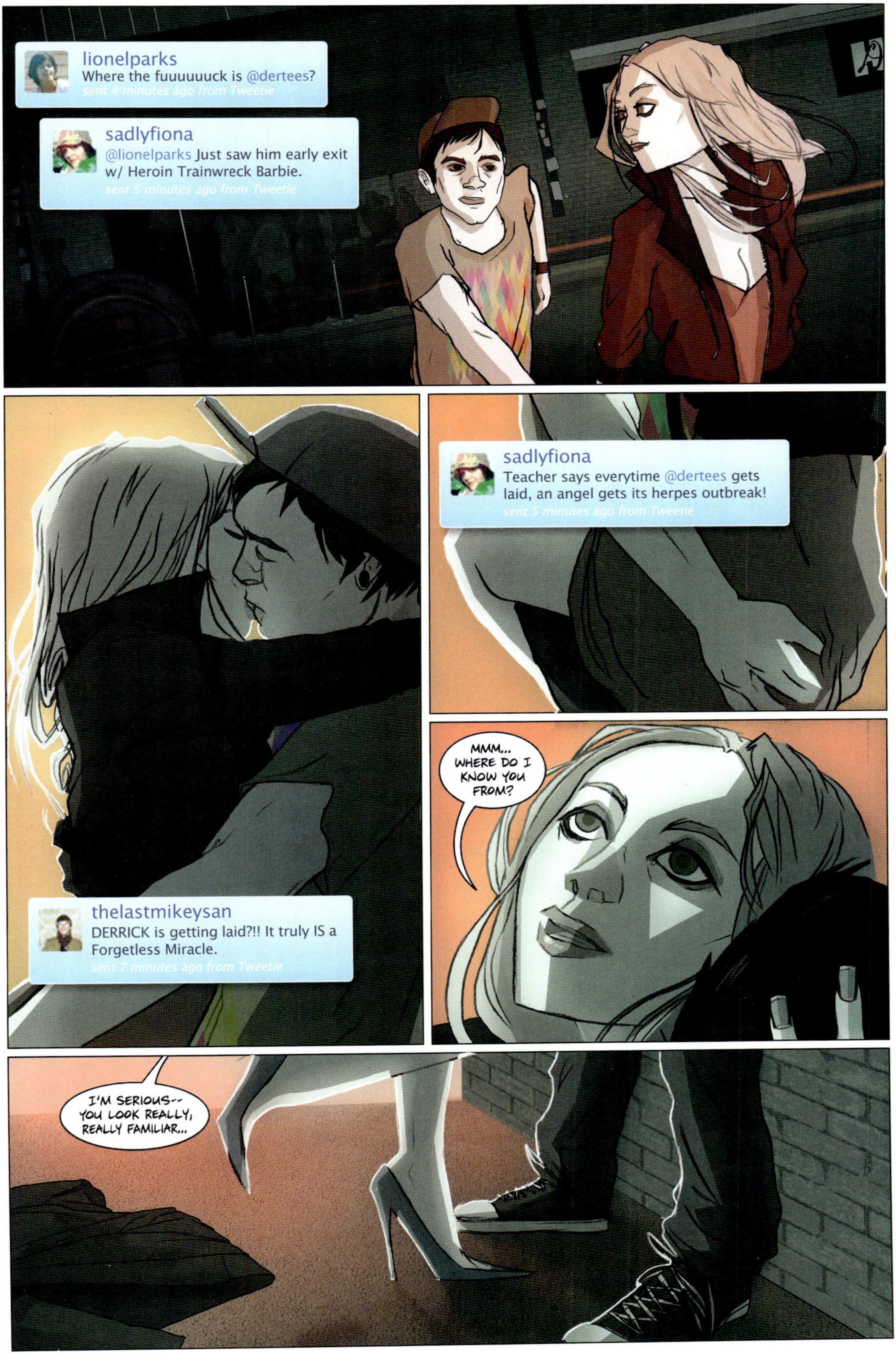
lionelparks
Where the fuuuuuuck is @dertees?
sent 4 minutes ago from Tweetie
sadlyfiona
@lionelparks Just saw him early exit w/ Heroin Trainwreck Barbie.
sent 5 minutes ago from Tweetie
thelastmikeysan
DERRICK is getting laid?!! It truly IS a Forgetless Miracle.
sent 7 minutes ago from Tweetie
sadlyfiona
Teacher says everytime @dertees gets laid, an angel gets its herpes outbreak!
sent 5 minutes ago from Tweetie
MMM... WHERE DO I KNOW YOU FROM?
I'M SERIOUS-- YOU LOOK REALLY, REALLY FAMILIAR...

30 MINUTES EARLIER...
ONE LITTLE MOVE, FUCKLY, AND I WILL BLOW YOUR NUTS OFF.
FUCKLY?

JESUS, SONIA, JUST SHOOT HIM ALREADY...
WAIT... DO YOU HEAR THAT?
HEAR WHAT?
THEY'RE STARTING. OR ENDING. WHATEVER. THE BAND'S OFF THE STAGE.
THEY'RE ON.
OH GOOD, A SENTIMENTAL HIPSTER...
OH COME ON. I MEAN, YOU GOTTA LOVE THE SYMMETRY HERE, RIGHT?
I'M GONNA DIE AT THE VERY LAST FORGETLESS.
YOU KNOW WHAT THAT MEANS, DON'T YOU?
I FUCKING AM FORGETLESS.

10 HOURS EARLIER...
WHAT THE FUCK IS FORGETLESS?
YOU KNOW WHAT FORGETLESS IS. YOU'VE BEEN. A BUNCH OF TIMES.
OH YEAH.
WELL... I LIKE TO PRETEND I DON'T.
IT'S THE LAST ONE. PEOPLE WILL EXPECT US TO BE THERE.
YOU KNOW, FOR POSTERITY.
POSTERITY? THE PICTURES GO UP ON FACEBOOK, NOT IN YOUR FUCKING HIGH SCHOOL YEARBOOK, SONIA.
OOH-- HOLD ON...
NO WAY--
--YOU ARE NOT ACTUALLY GOING TO EAT THE RAT FOOD?!!
I CAN'T WATCH YOU DO THIS TO YOURSELF, YOU FUCKING COW.
COME FIND ME IN TOP SHOP WHEN YOU'RE DONE.
SoSoSara
@SoniaLikely eats like my dad.
sent 45 seconds ago from Tweetie
SoniaLikely
@SoSoSara Is that why you're always begging me to touch you down there?
sent 7 seconds ago from Tweetie

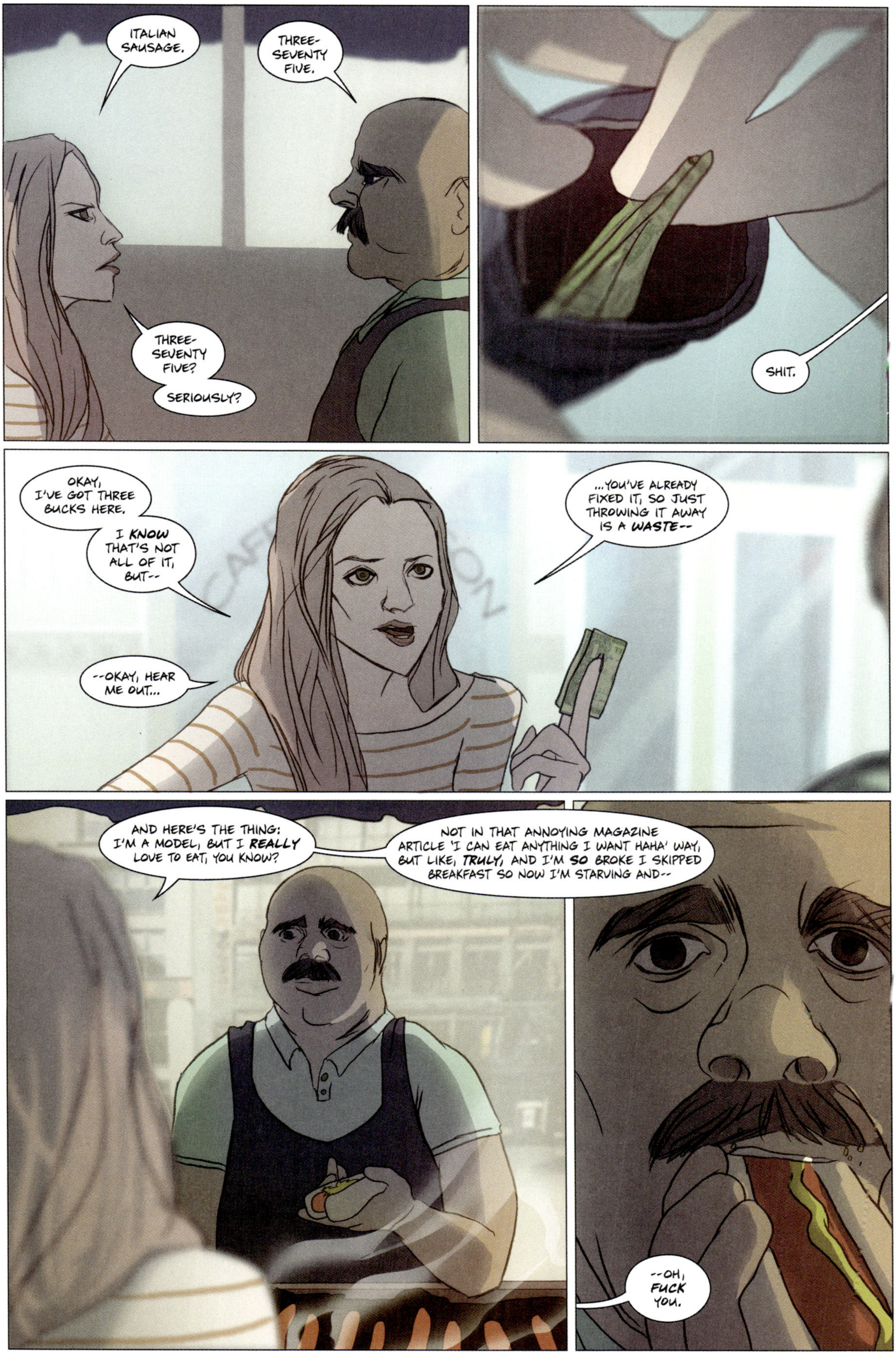
ITALIAN SAUSAGE.
THREE-SEVENTY FIVE.
THREE-SEVENTY FIVE?
SERIOUSLY?
SHIT.
OKAY, I'VE GOT THREE BUCKS HERE.
I KNOW THAT'S NOT ALL OF IT, BUT--
--OKAY, HEAR ME OUT...
...YOU'VE ALREADY FIXED IT, SO JUST THROWING IT AWAY IS A WASTE--
AND HERE'S THE THING: I'M A MODEL, BUT I REALLY LOVE TO EAT, YOU KNOW?
NOT IN THAT ANNOYING MAGAZINE ARTICLE 'I CAN EAT ANYTHING I WANT HAHA' WAY, BUT LIKE, TRULY, AND I'M SO BROKE I SKIPPED BREAKFAST SO NOW I'M STARVING AND--
--OH, FUCK YOU.

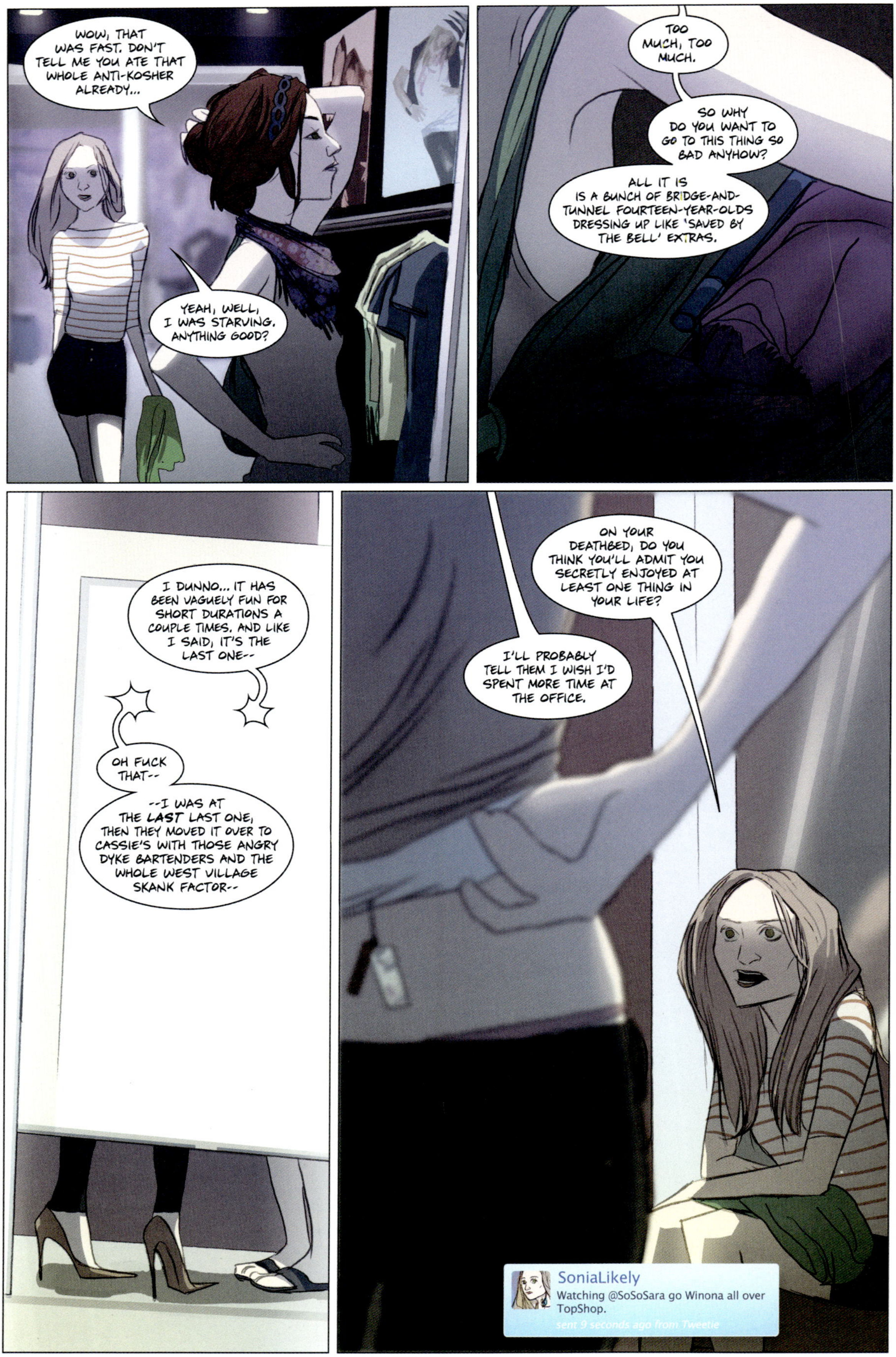
WOW, THAT WAS FAST. DON'T TELL ME YOU ATE THAT WHOLE ANTI-KOSHER ALREADY...
YEAH, WELL, I WAS STARVING. ANYTHING GOOD?
TOO MUCH, TOO MUCH.
SO WHY DO YOU WANT TO GO TO THIS THING SO BAD ANYHOW?
ALL IT IS IS A BUNCH OF BRIDGE-AND-TUNNEL FOURTEEN-YEAR-OLDS DRESSING UP LIKE 'SAVED BY THE BELL' EXTRAS.
I DUNNO... IT HAS BEEN VAGUELY FUN FOR SHORT DURATIONS A COUPLE TIMES. AND LIKE I SAID, IT'S THE LAST ONE--
OH FUCK THAT--
--I WAS AT THE LAST LAST ONE, THEN THEY MOVED IT OVER TO CASSIE'S WITH THOSE ANGRY DYKE BARTENDERS AND THE WHOLE WEST VILLAGE SKANK FACTOR--
ON YOUR DEATHBED, DO YOU THINK YOU'LL ADMIT YOU SECRETLY ENJOYED AT LEAST ONE THING IN YOUR LIFE?
I'LL PROBABLY TELL THEM I WISH I'D SPENT MORE TIME AT THE OFFICE.
SoniaLikely
Watching @SoSoSara go Winona all over TopShop.
sent 9 seconds ago from Tweetie

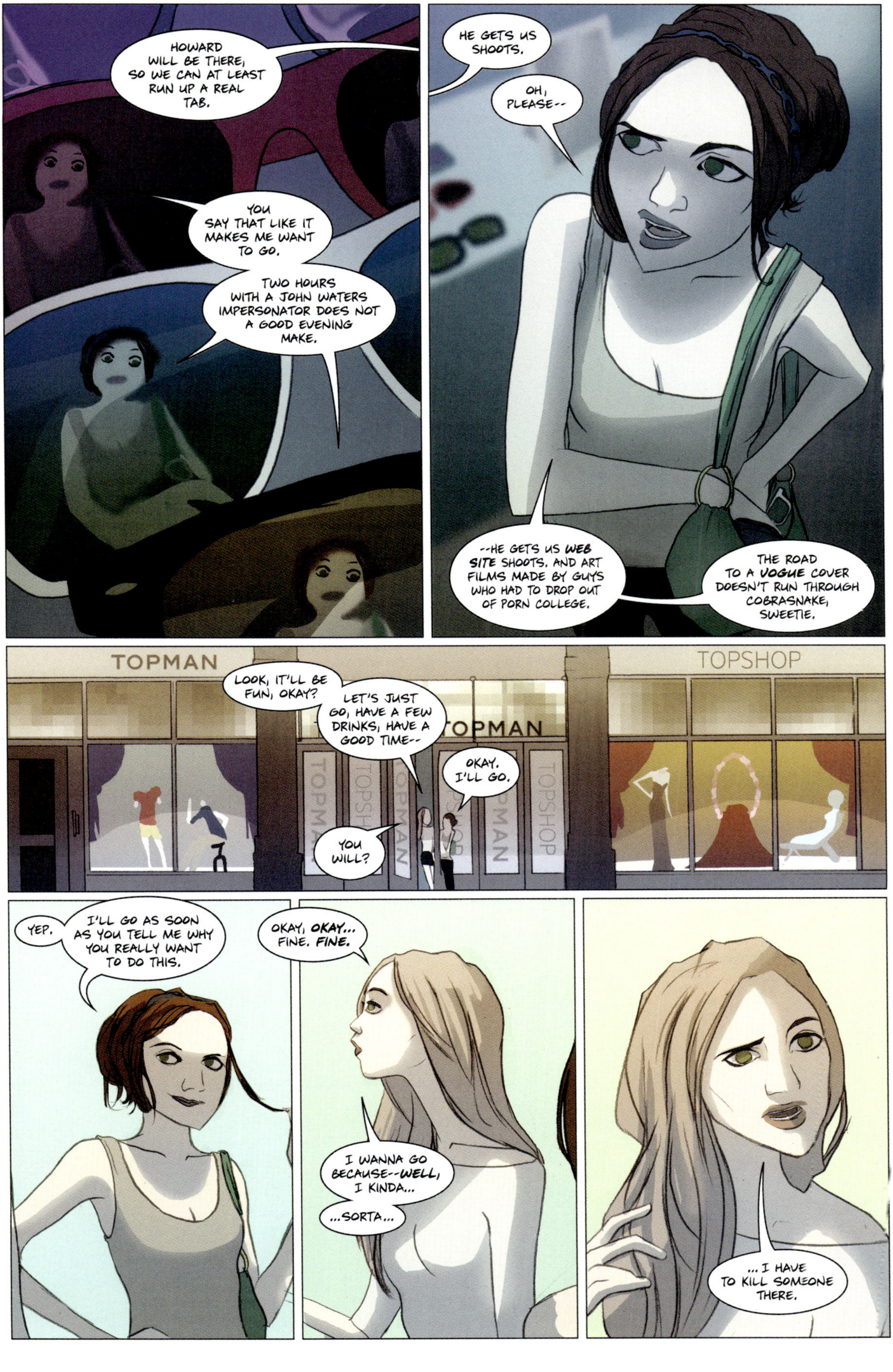
HOWARD WILL BE THERE, SO WE CAN AT LEAST RUN UP A REAL TAB.
YOU SAY THAT LIKE IT MAKES ME WANT TO GO.
TWO HOURS WITH A JOHN WATERS IMPERSONATOR DOES NOT A GOOD EVENING MAKE.
HE GETS US SHOOTS.
OH, PLEASE--
--HE GETS US **WEB SITE** SHOOTS. AND ART FILMS MADE BY GUYS WHO HAD TO DROP OUT OF PORN COLLEGE.
THE ROAD TO A **VOGUE** COVER DOESN'T RUN THROUGH COBRASNAKE, SWEETIE.
TOPMAN
TOPSHOP
LOOK, IT'LL BE FUN, OKAY?
LET'S JUST GO, HAVE A FEW DRINKS, HAVE A GOOD TIME--
OKAY. I'LL GO.
YOU WILL?
YEP.
I'LL GO AS SOON AS YOU TELL ME WHY YOU REALLY WANT TO DO THIS.
OKAY, **OKAY**... FINE. **FINE.**
I WANNA GO BECAUSE--**WELL**, I KINDA...
...SORTA...
...I HAVE TO KILL SOMEONE THERE.

24 HOURS EARLIER...
CALM DOWN. YOU JUST NEED TO LOOK PROFESSIONAL.
I DO THE TALKING.
I'M FINE.
THERE WE ARE...SORRY TO KEEP YOU BOTH WAITING!
SoniaLikely
A lot of cock in this house. @sososara would probably chip a tooth!
sent 2 seconds ago from Tweetie
THAT'S NO PROBLEM. YOU HAVE A LOVELY PLACE HERE, MA'AM.
PLEASE, CALL ME MINDY.
SHE DOESN'T LOOK LIKE MUCH.
ALEX!

IT'S ALL RIGHT, MINDY. I HAPPEN TO AGREE WITH YOUR HUSBAND.
OUR OPERATIVES DON'T LOOK LIKE OPERATIVES. THAT'S WHAT ALLOWS THEM TO DO THEIR JOBS WITH MINIMAL INTERFERENCE.
BUT I ASSURE YOU, THIS IS ONE OF OUR MOST CAPABLE AGENTS. SHE **WILL** TAKE CARE OF YOUR PROBLEM.
YEAH, WHAT **IS** YOUR PROBLEM?
EXCUSE ME?
AM I ALLOWED TO ASK THAT?
I THINK WHAT SHE MEANS IS, WHAT INFORMATION CAN YOU GIVE US IN TERMS OF THE CONTRACT?
THE CONTRACT? OH...UH, NOT MUCH.
511 GREENWICH
11:00 PM
WE DON'T EVEN KNOW HIS NAME. WE JUST HAVE THIS PICTURE MY WIFE TOOK, AND WE KNOW HE'S GOING TO BE AT THIS-- THIS PARTY, IT'S CALLED **FORGETLESS.**
YOU KNOW IT?
I'M... **AWARE** OF IT.
FINE.
OKAY, SO THIS IS HIM AND HE'S GONNA BE THERE.
WHY DO YOU WANT HIM... **YOU KNOW?**

EXCUSE ME?
HONEY, WE DON'T HAVE TO--
NO, NO, IT'S FINE.
IF YOU MUST KNOW, THIS MAN...THIS MAN...
...THIS MAN RAPED OUR DAUGHTER!
OKAY.
OKAY, WHAT?
OKAY, I'M IN. LET'S GO.
SoniaLikely
Got a new job today, wish me luck!
sent 15 seconds ago from Tweetie

"WHY DO YOU WANT HIM...YOU KNOW?"
"ONE OF OUR MOST CAPABLE AGENTS"?
ARE YOU FUCKING KIDDING ME?
MAYBE I SHOULD GO BACK UP THERE AND TELL HIM THIS IS YOUR FIRST TIME, THEN.
YOU THINK HE'LL STILL PAY?
LOOK, NO ONE IS FORCING YOU TO DO THIS. YOU CAME TO US, REMEMBER?
NO...NO. I'LL DO IT.
I HAD MY PROM NIGHT RUINED, TOO, I CAN--
NO, DON'T DO THAT, EITHER. MAKE THIS A JOB, YOU UNDERSTAND? YOU MOVE A FINGER, SOMETHING GOES OFF, SOMEONE STOPS MOVING, YOU START LEAVING.
GOT IT?
DON'T BRING YOUR PERSONAL SHIT INTO--
STOP! I GOT IT, OKAY? I GOT IT.
I DON'T GET YOU, SONIA. WHY ARE YOU MAKING THIS SO HARD?
I MEAN, WHY CAN'T YOU BE MORE LIKE SARA?

33 HOURS LATER...
AND THEN, BLAM BLAM BLAM BLAM!
AT LEAST FOUR. SOMETIMES SIX, IF THEY'RE FAT.
YOU GOTTA MAKE SURE, YOU KNOW?
STRICT NO REFUNDS POLICY AND ALL THAT.
I'M SO PROUD OF YOU, SWEETIE! I TOLD YOU THIS WAS THE WAY TO GO. I'VE BEEN MAKING SO MUCH MONEY KILLING THESE ASSHOLES I DON'T EVEN NEED SHOOTS--
FOR FUCK'S SAKE, SARA--THE CABBIE CAN HEAR YOU, YOU KNOW!
OH, JESUS CHRIST, ARE YOU SERIOUS?
HEY, DRIVER, WHERE YOU FROM?
HAITI.
SEE?
WHERE THAT GUY'S FROM, THEY KILL PEOPLE ALL THE TIME, FOR A HELLUVA LOT LESS MONEY THAN YOU'VE GOT.
IS TRUE! WE DO!
THANK YOU.
NOW COME ON, PRINCESS. WE'RE HERE.

MY FRIENDS ARE ALREADY IN THERE!
I'M ROOMMATES WITH ONE OF THE BARTENDERS!
I GOTTA POOP!
HEY RAYMOND.
I NEED A DRINK.
EXIT
DAMN RIGHT, YOU DO. YOU'RE SO NERVOUS YOUR NIPPLES ARE SHOWING.
YOU NEED TO CHILL THE FUCK OUT, SWEETIE.
THIS'LL BE EASY, I PROMISE. WE'RE GONNA FIND THIS GUY, TAKE HIM SOMEPLACE NICE AND QUIET, AND JUST--

ONE HOUR LATER...
SHOOT HIM, FOR FUCK'S SAKE!
WOULD YOU STOP? YOU'RE GETTING ON MY NERVES WITH THAT SHIT.
THEN CLOSE YOUR EYES AND PRETEND YOU'RE KILLING ME.
BUT JUST GET IT **OVER** WITH.
"I FUCKING **AM** FORGETLESS."
JESUS CHRIST, LOOK AT HIM. HE'S WEARING **GAUGES.**
GODDAMN IT...
...WHY'D YOU DO IT?
WHAT?
SONIA, NO--
UM, EXCUSE ME...
...DO WHAT?
OKAY, FINE.
WE'LL PLAY "ASK THE RAPIST."
HEY, UNDERDRESSER, WHY'D YOU NON-CONSENSUAL ON THE UPPER WEST SIDE LAST WEEK?

WHY DID I...
...NO WAY, YOU GOTTA BE FUCKING KIDDING ME--
--THAT'S WHY YOU'RE HERE?
THAT?!!
OH, NOW THAT IS JUST HI-LARIOUS...
LOOK AT HIM! HE THINKS THIS IS FUNNY?!!
GIMME THE GUN, I'LL DO IT--
NO, I'VE GOT IT, I--
LIVE FROM ABN STUDIOS IN NEW YORK!!! IT'S--
DO NOT ENTER
OH. HEY.

IS THAT A GUN?
IS THAT A KOALA?
HEY!
YOU LITTLE FUCKER! I'M GONNA--
JUST LET ME--
GET OFF ME--I--
BLAM!!!

3 DAYS EARLIER...
SHIT!!!
HAHA, CALM DOWN, DICKFACE, IT'S JUST A WATER GUN...
THANK CHRIST--
...THAT I FILLED WITH MY URINE.
YOU SICK FUCK!
AT LEAST YOU'RE UP NOW.
COME ON, WE GOTTA GO.
GO WHERE?
IDIOTAROD DRILL ISN'T 'TIL FIVE.
I NEED AN ASSISTANT.
GUNTHER'S SYPHILIS IS ACTING UP OR SOMETHING. I GOTTA HANDLE HIS APPOINTMENTS.

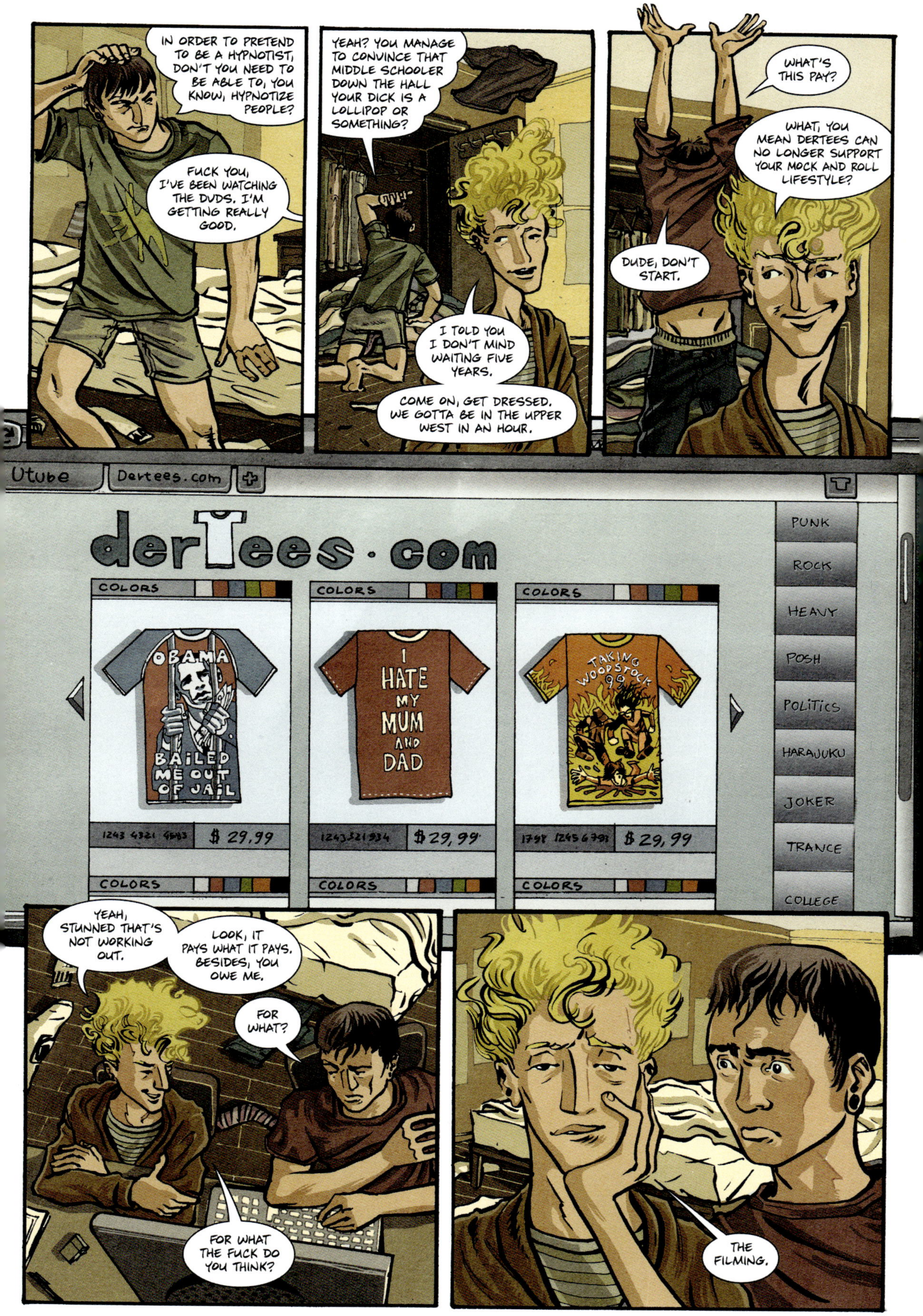
IN ORDER TO PRETEND TO BE A HYPNOTIST, DON'T YOU NEED TO BE ABLE TO, YOU KNOW, HYPNOTIZE PEOPLE?
FUCK YOU, I'VE BEEN WATCHING THE DVDS. I'M GETTING REALLY GOOD.
YEAH? YOU MANAGE TO CONVINCE THAT MIDDLE SCHOOLER DOWN THE HALL YOUR DICK IS A LOLLIPOP OR SOMETHING?
I TOLD YOU I DON'T MIND WAITING FIVE YEARS.
COME ON, GET DRESSED. WE GOTTA BE IN THE UPPER WEST IN AN HOUR.
WHAT'S THIS PAY?
WHAT, YOU MEAN DERTEES CAN NO LONGER SUPPORT YOUR MOCK AND ROLL LIFESTYLE?
DUDE, DON'T START.
Utube
Dertees.com
derTees.com
PUNK
ROCK
HEAVY
POSH
POLITICS
HARAJUKU
JOKER
TRANCE
COLLEGE
COLORS
OBAMA BAILED ME OUT OF JAIL
$ 29.99
COLORS
I HATE MY MUM AND DAD
$ 29,99
COLORS
TAKING WOODSTOCK 99
$ 29,99
COLORS
COLORS
COLORS
YEAH, STUNNED THAT'S NOT WORKING OUT.
LOOK, IT PAYS WHAT IT PAYS. BESIDES, YOU OWE ME.
FOR WHAT?
FOR WHAT THE FUCK DO YOU THINK?
THE FILMING.

OKAY, UH, HELLO, I'M JASON, AND THIS HERE--THIS IS MY FRIEND DERRICK.
350
'SUP, AMERICA!
LittleMissFirehead (46 seconds ago)
This guy looks stupid
AND WE'RE STANDING IN FRONT OF THE EMPIRE STATE BUILDING, CROWN JEWEL OF THE NEW YORK CITY TOURISM INDUSTRY.
ROUGHLY A HALF MILLION PEOPLE VISIT THIS BUILDING EACH YEAR, BEST KNOWN FOR ITS USAGE IN THE 1934 CLASSIC, KING KONG. VISITORS LOVE TO GO TO THE TOP AND ENJOY ITS MAJESTIC VIEW OF THE CITY!
EMPIRE STATE
ske91 (34 seconds ago)
I went there with my mom when I was 10!
BUT TODAY, WE'RE VISITING FOR A VERY DIFFERENT REASON, AREN'T WE?
YUP. HEY, DID YOU REMEMBER THE UMBRELLA FOR COVER?
Darkleh615 (21 seconds ago)
I didn't think cialis would work for me but then I tried this web site-- cheap prescription meds for under ten dollars.
WHY DON'T YOU TELL EVERYONE OUT THERE WHAT YOU'RE PLANNING TO DO TODAY, DERRICK?
I'M GONNA FUCK IT.
Gamestabber (3 seconds ago)
Wat

THAT'S RIGHT, DEAR VIEWERS, WE'RE ABOUT TO WITNESS HISTORY BEING MADE--THE EMPIRE STATE BUILDING, THAT PROUD MONUMENT TO CIVIC VIRTUE, IS ABOUT TO LOSE HER CHERRY. DERRICK HAS IDENTIFIED A SMALL VENTILATION HOLE--
IT'S NOT THAT SMALL!
IHAZO (1 minute ago)
AHAHAHA I can't believe this! Is this real?
OKAY AND WE'RE OFF! NOT SINCE DAVID COPPERFIELD MADE THE STATUE OF LIBERTY DISAPPEAR HAS NEW YORK BEEN PART OF SUCH A STUNNING SPECTACLE--DUDE, MOVE THE UMBRELLA!
I'M TRYING TO CONCENTRATE!
RoundHal32 (43 seconds ago)
WHAT IS WRONG WITH WHITE PEOPLE
SCHOOL FIELD TRIPS, SENIORS, PEOPLE FROM ALL WALKS AND WAYS OF LIFE ARE HERE TO ADMIRE THIS MOMENTOUS OCCASION, WITH--SHIT, DERRICK! DERRICK! COPS!
NOT FAIR!
reverseforwards2 (38 seconds ago)
These people need to find Jesus and soon. This kind of perversity is a sin in the eyes of God. 'And even as they did not like to retain God in their knowledge, God gave them over to a reprobate mind, to do those things which are not convenient' Romans 1:28
WELL, THE DEED IS DONE, FIFTH AVENUE WILL NEVER BE THE SAME AND--HUFF, HUFF--DARE I SAY, NEITHER WILL OUR FRIEND DERRICK!
I HAD SEX WITH A BUILDING!
DeadSalesman (14 seconds ago)
This shit is hilarious. My gf and I couldn't stop loling.

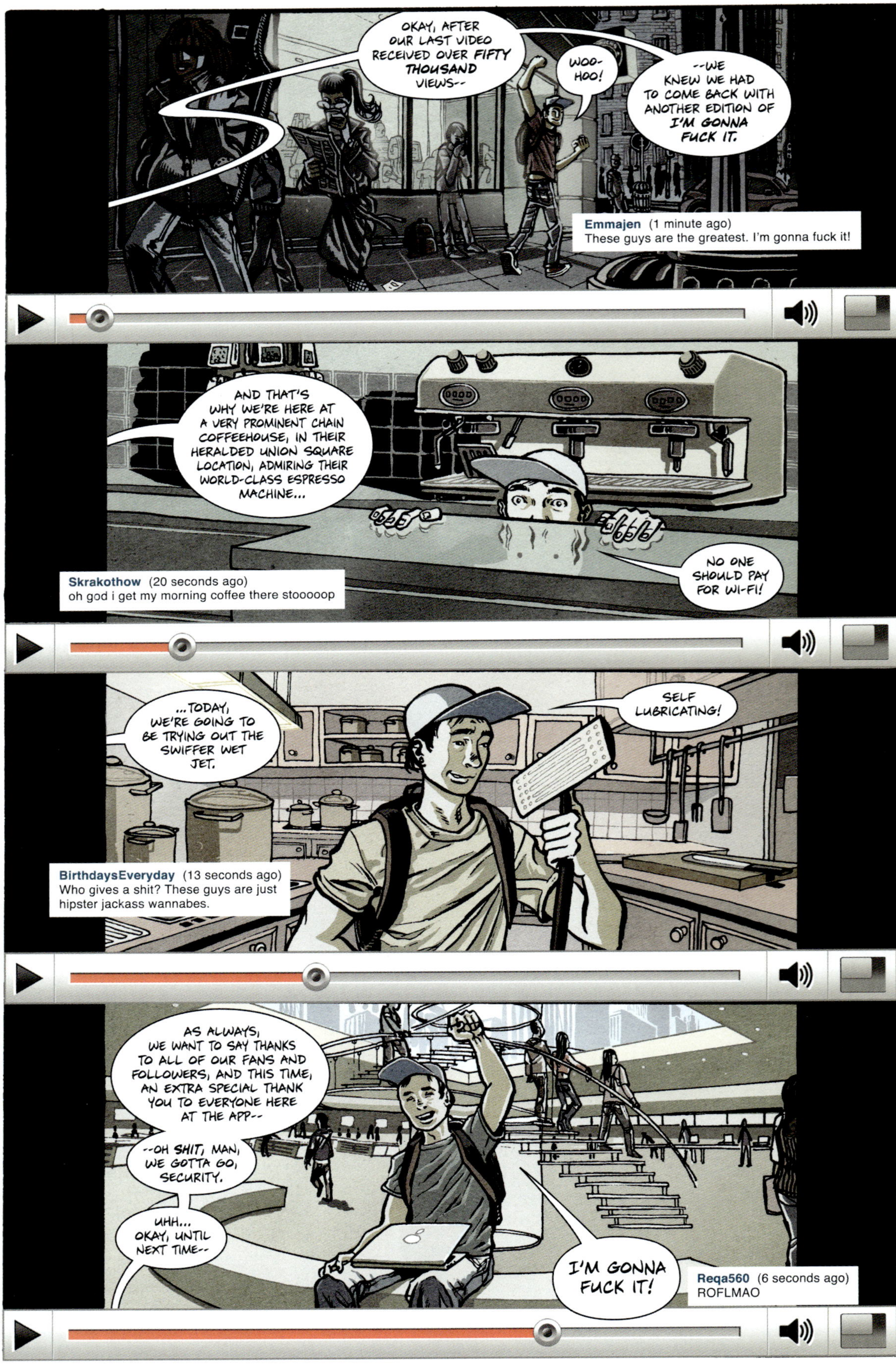
OKAY, AFTER OUR LAST VIDEO RECEIVED OVER FIFTY THOUSAND VIEWS--
WOO-HOO!
--WE KNEW WE HAD TO COME BACK WITH ANOTHER EDITION OF I'M GONNA FUCK IT.
Emmajen (1 minute ago)
These guys are the greatest. I'm gonna fuck it!
AND THAT'S WHY WE'RE HERE AT A VERY PROMINENT CHAIN COFFEEHOUSE, IN THEIR HERALDED UNION SQUARE LOCATION, ADMIRING THEIR WORLD-CLASS ESPRESSO MACHINE...
NO ONE SHOULD PAY FOR WI-FI!
Skrakothow (20 seconds ago)
oh god i get my morning coffee there stooooop
...TODAY, WE'RE GOING TO BE TRYING OUT THE SWIFFER WET JET.
SELF LUBRICATING!
BirthdaysEveryday (13 seconds ago)
Who gives a shit? These guys are just hipster jackass wannabes.
AS ALWAYS, WE WANT TO SAY THANKS TO ALL OF OUR FANS AND FOLLOWERS, AND THIS TIME, AN EXTRA SPECIAL THANK YOU TO EVERYONE HERE AT THE APP--
--OH SHIT, MAN, WE GOTTA GO, SECURITY.
UHH... OKAY, UNTIL NEXT TIME--
I'M GONNA FUCK IT!
Reqa560 (6 seconds ago)
ROFLMAO

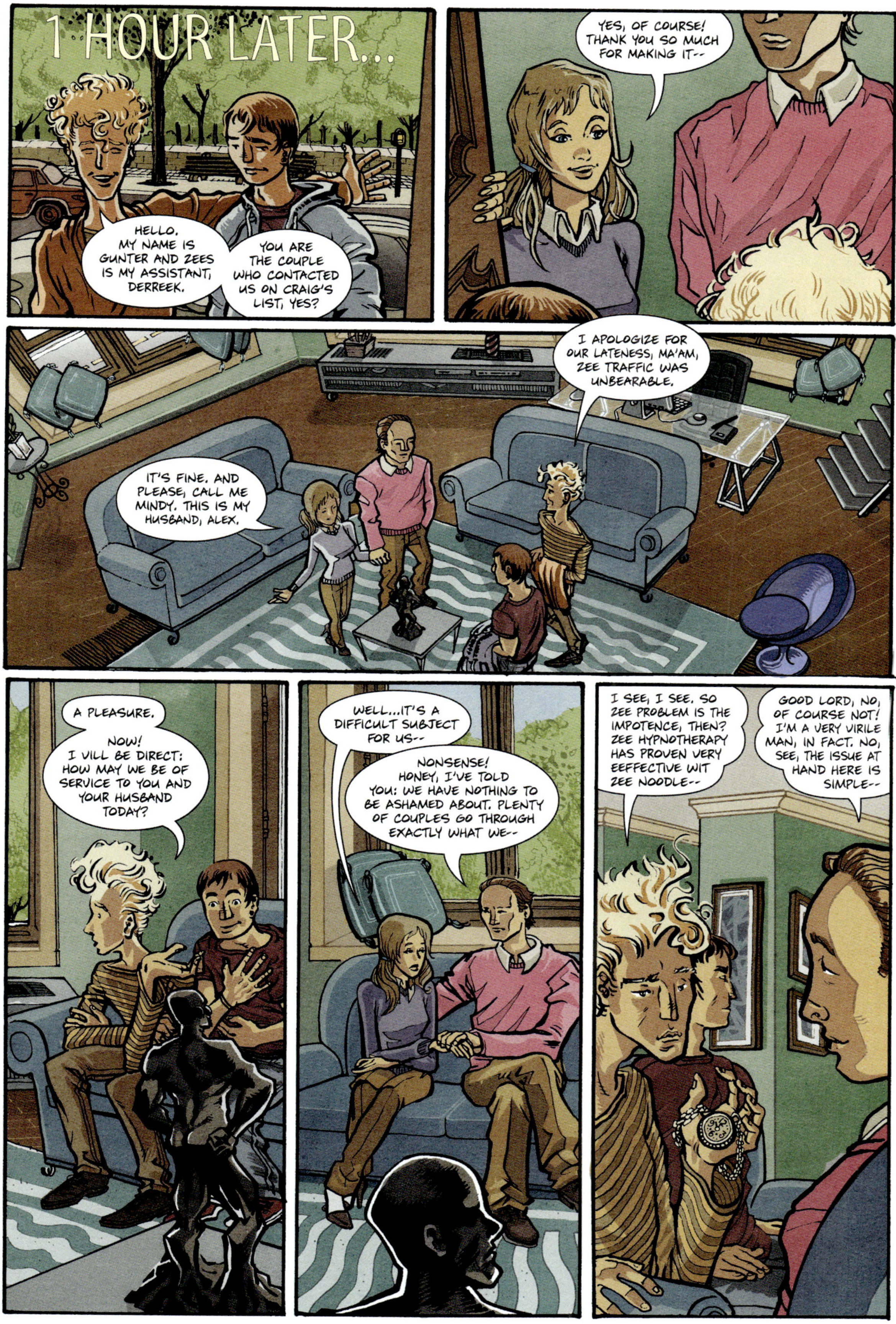
1 HOUR LATER...
HELLO. MY NAME IS GUNTER AND ZEES IS MY ASSISTANT, DERREEK.
YOU ARE THE COUPLE WHO CONTACTED US ON CRAIG'S LIST, YES?
YES, OF COURSE! THANK YOU SO MUCH FOR MAKING IT--
I APOLOGIZE FOR OUR LATENESS, MA'AM, ZEE TRAFFIC WAS UNBEARABLE.
IT'S FINE. AND PLEASE, CALL ME MINDY. THIS IS MY HUSBAND, ALEX.
A PLEASURE.
NOW! I VILL BE DIRECT: HOW MAY WE BE OF SERVICE TO YOU AND YOUR HUSBAND TODAY?
WELL...IT'S A DIFFICULT SUBJECT FOR US--
NONSENSE! HONEY, I'VE TOLD YOU: WE HAVE NOTHING TO BE ASHAMED ABOUT. PLENTY OF COUPLES GO THROUGH EXACTLY WHAT WE--
I SEE, I SEE. SO ZEE PROBLEM IS THE IMPOTENCE, THEN? ZEE HYPNOTHERAPY HAS PROVEN VERY EEFFECTIVE WIT ZEE NOODLE--
GOOD LORD, NO, OF COURSE NOT! I'M A VERY VIRILE MAN, IN FACT. NO, SEE, THE ISSUE AT HAND HERE IS SIMPLE--

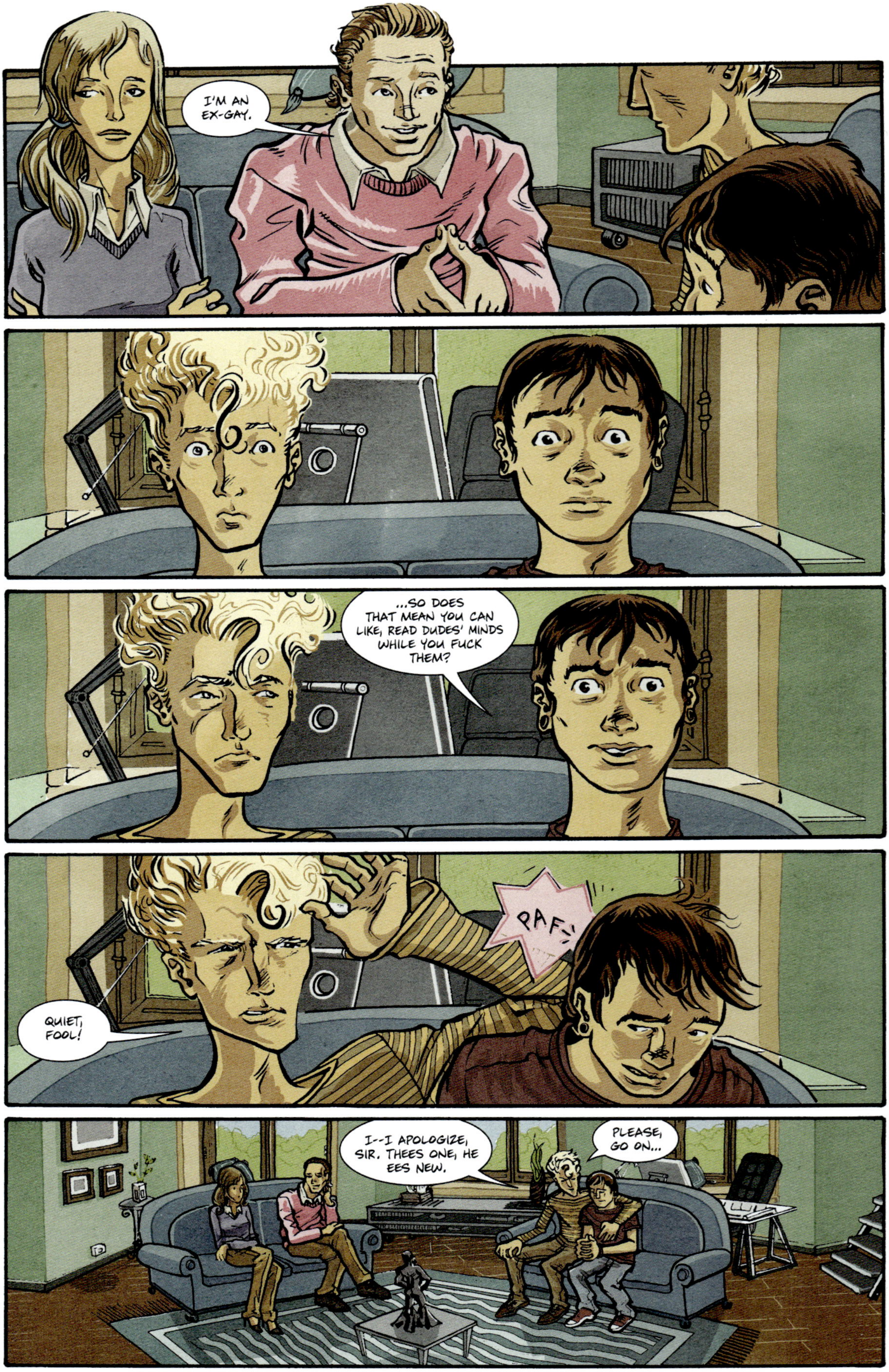
I'M AN EX-GAY.
...SO DOES THAT MEAN YOU CAN LIKE, READ DUDES' MINDS WHILE YOU FUCK THEM?
PAF!
QUIET, FOOL!
I--I APOLOGIZE, SIR. THEES ONE, HE EES NEW.
PLEASE, GO ON...

NO, IT'S FINE. I'M USED TO THAT KIND OF IGNORANCE, ESPECIALLY HERE IN THIS CITY.
YOU SEE, I HAD BEEN A MEMBER OF THE HOMOSEXUAL LIFESTYLE SINCE I WAS TWELVE YEARS OLD.
THEN, EIGHT YEARS AGO, WITH THE HELP OF MY FAMILY, I ACCEPTED JESUS CHRIST AS MY LORD AND PERSONAL SAVIOR.
TWO WEEKS LATER, I MET MINDY, AND THREE MONTHS AFTER THAT, WE WERE MARRIED--
--IT WAS A BEAUTIFUL CEREMONY--
--AND NOW JESUS IS THE ONLY MAN I NEED IN MY LIFE.
AH-- I SEE, I SEE...
SO, VAT IS IT YOU NEED US FOR, THEN?
WELL... TEMPTATION IS AN UNFORTUNATE PART OF LIFE, AND NOW THAT WE HAVE A DAUGHTER--
A DAUGHTER?
THAT'S RIGHT. WE'VE RECENTLY ADOPTED.
HER NAME IS ALLISON. ALEX HAD WANTED A BABY, BUT I CONVINCED HIM WE COULD DO MORE GOOD BY TAKING IN AN OLDER CHILD--
SHE'S THE LIGHT OF OUR LIFE. WE WANT TO DO RIGHT BY HER, AND THAT MEANS SETTING THE PROPER EXAMPLE OURSELVES. IT'S BEEN HARD ENOUGH SINCE MY WORK SENT US HERE TO NEW YORK--
ALEX IS A SEGMENT PRODUCER FOR FOX NEWS.

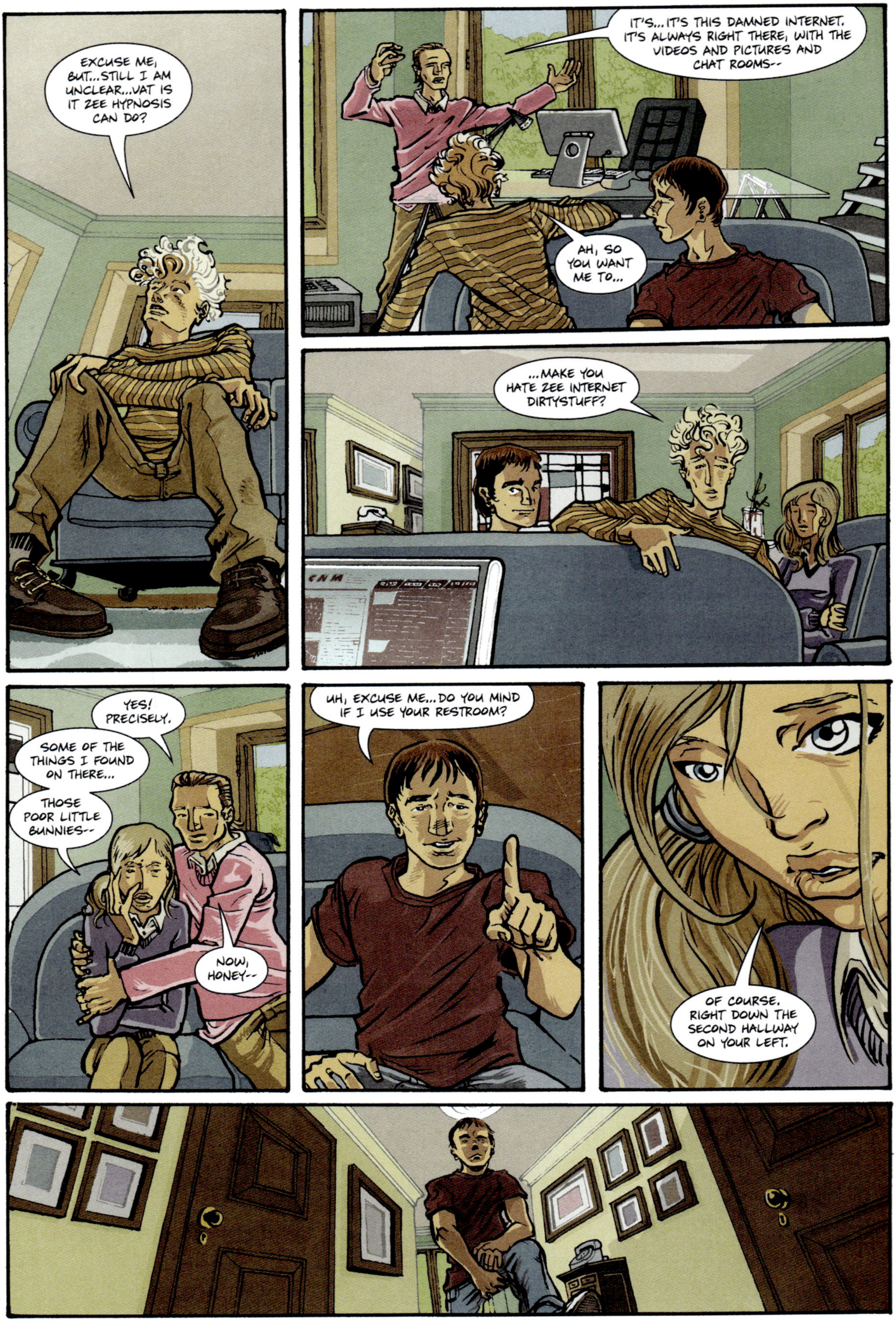
EXCUSE ME, BUT...STILL I AM UNCLEAR...VAT IS IT ZEE HYPNOSIS CAN DO?
IT'S... IT'S THIS DAMNED INTERNET. IT'S ALWAYS RIGHT THERE, WITH THE VIDEOS AND PICTURES AND CHAT ROOMS--
AH, SO YOU WANT ME TO...
...MAKE YOU HATE ZEE INTERNET DIRTYSTUFF?
YES! PRECISELY.
SOME OF THE THINGS I FOUND ON THERE...
THOSE POOR LITTLE BUNNIES--
NOW, HONEY--
UH, EXCUSE ME...DO YOU MIND IF I USE YOUR RESTROOM?
OF COURSE. RIGHT DOWN THE SECOND HALLWAY ON YOUR LEFT.

OH, SORRY! I WAS LOOKING FOR THE--
--HOLY SHIT.
ALL RIGHTEE...ZEE PROCESS IS VERY EASY, I NEED YOU TO BEGIN TO RELAX, ALEX, AND--
BZZT!
--EH, EXCUSE ME--
Derrick
dude you have to come see this now
AHEM, IF YOU WILL...UMM... PARDON ME FOR ZEE MOMENT, MY ASSISTANT... AHH... HE EES HAVING SOME DIFFICULTIES...
...AH, YES, YES... HE IS JUST A BIT ILL AND I HAVE HIS MEDEECATION...
ERR...
...BACK IN A JIFFY--

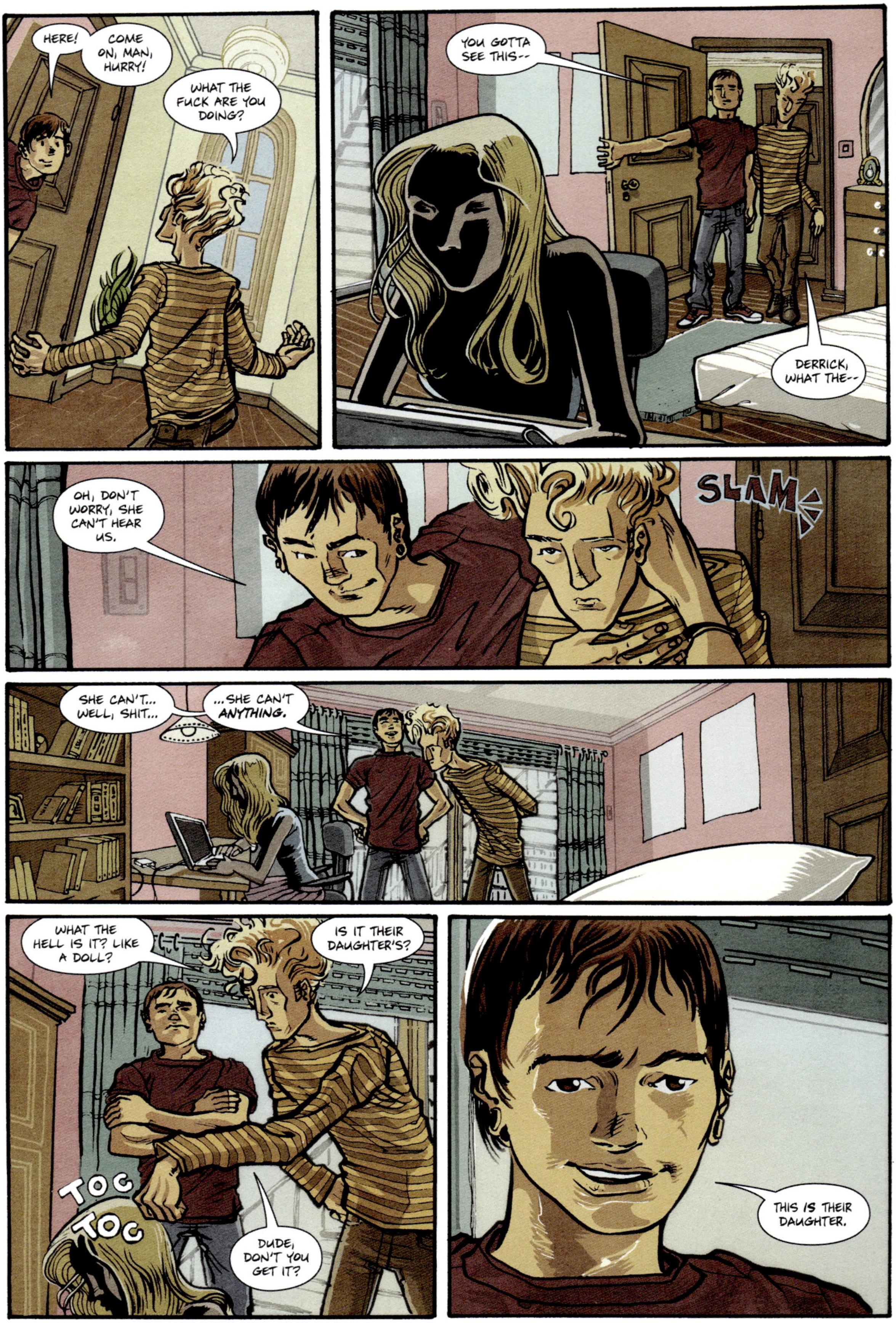
HERE!
COME ON, MAN, HURRY!
WHAT THE FUCK ARE YOU DOING?
YOU GOTTA SEE THIS--
DERRICK, WHAT THE--
OH, DON'T WORRY, SHE CAN'T HEAR US.
SLAM
SHE CAN'T... WELL, SHIT...
...SHE CAN'T ANYTHING.
WHAT THE HELL IS IT? LIKE A DOLL?
IS IT THEIR DAUGHTER'S?
TOC TOC
DUDE, DON'T YOU GET IT?
THIS IS THEIR DAUGHTER.

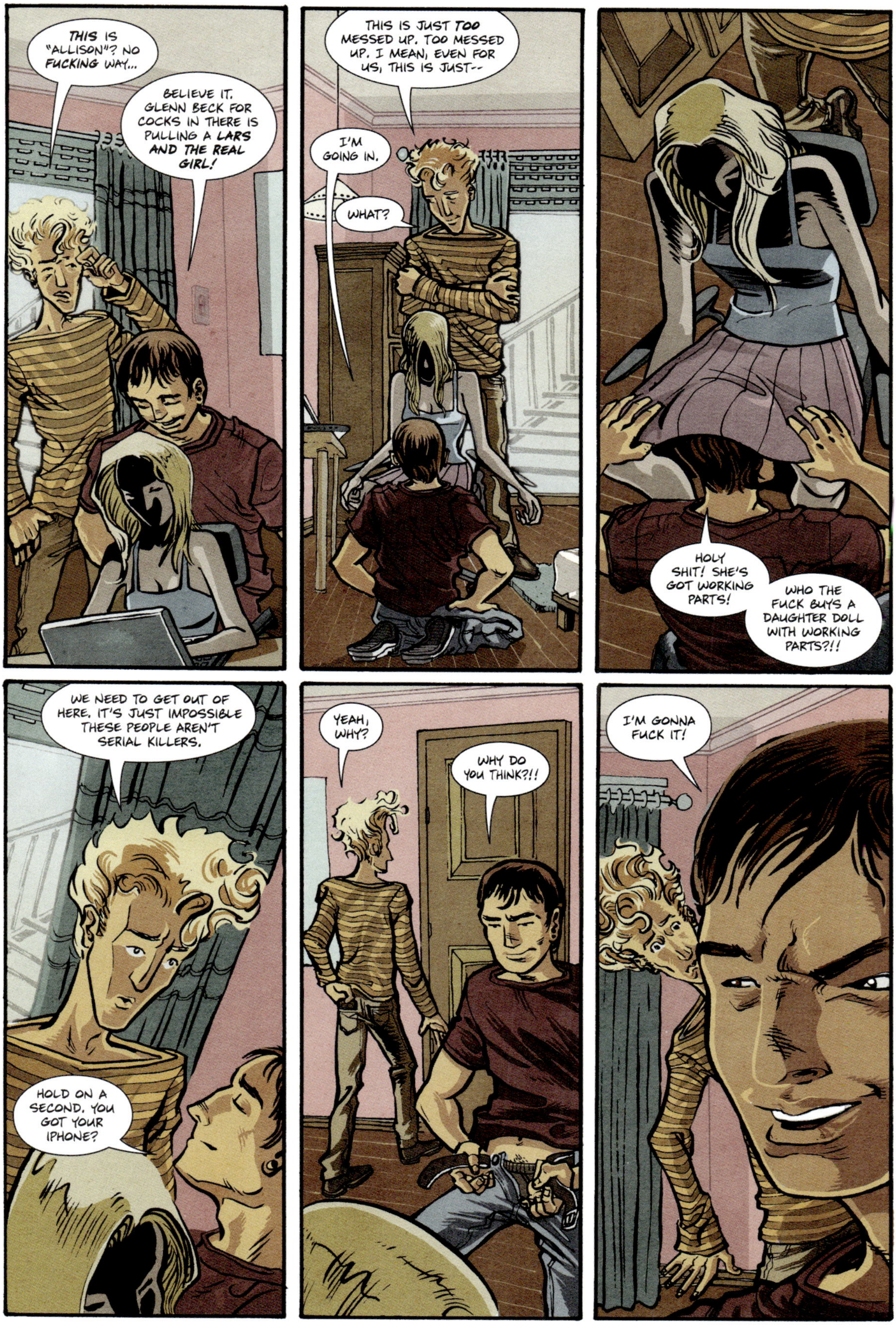
THIS IS "ALLISON"? NO FUCKING WAY...
BELIEVE IT. GLENN BECK FOR COCKS IN THERE IS PULLING A LARS AND THE REAL GIRL!
THIS IS JUST TOO MESSED UP. TOO MESSED UP. I MEAN, EVEN FOR US, THIS IS JUST--
I'M GOING IN.
WHAT?
HOLY SHIT! SHE'S GOT WORKING PARTS!
WHO THE FUCK BUYS A DAUGHTER DOLL WITH WORKING PARTS?!!
WE NEED TO GET OUT OF HERE. IT'S JUST IMPOSSIBLE THESE PEOPLE AREN'T SERIAL KILLERS.
HOLD ON A SECOND. YOU GOT YOUR IPHONE?
YEAH, WHY?
WHY DO YOU THINK?!!
I'M GONNA FUCK IT!

OKAY, SO, HEY, THIS IS JASON AGAIN, AND TODAY, WE'RE BROADCASTING FROM SOMEWHERE NEAR COLUMBUS CIRCLE, WITH A VERY SPECIAL SURPRISE EDITION--
--TODAY, DERRICK IS GOING TO BE FUCKING WHAT'S TYPICALLY REFERRED TO, I BELIEVE, AS A LIFE MODEL.
NOW, WHAT'S SO SPECIAL ABOUT HIM PLUGGING A BLOW-UP DOLL, YOU ASK?
WELL, THIS PARTICULAR DOLL HAPPENS TO BE THE PRETEND "DAUGHTER" OF A PROMINENT FOX NEWS PRODUCER WHO IS ACTUALLY IN THE NEXT ROOM--
--SO, THE STAKES ARE PRETTY HIGH HERE, AS DERRICK ATTEMPTS TO STRIKE BACK AT FUNDIE TEABAGGING HATEMONGERS IN THE PLACE THEY HOLD MOST DEAR--
--THEIR DAUGHTERS' PLASTIC VAGINAS.
HELLO, INTERWEBS! MY NAME IS ALLISON, AND I'M SOOOOO HORNY RIGHT NOW!
NOW THIS ONE HAS AN EXTRA-HIGH DANGER LEVEL. AGAIN, THEY ARE RIGHT IN THE NEXT ROOM-- BUT LUCKY FOR US, AS WE ALL KNOW BY NOW, DERRICK IS BOTH QUIET AND QUICK IN THE SACK.
IT'S TRUE. I FUCK LIKE A NINJA.

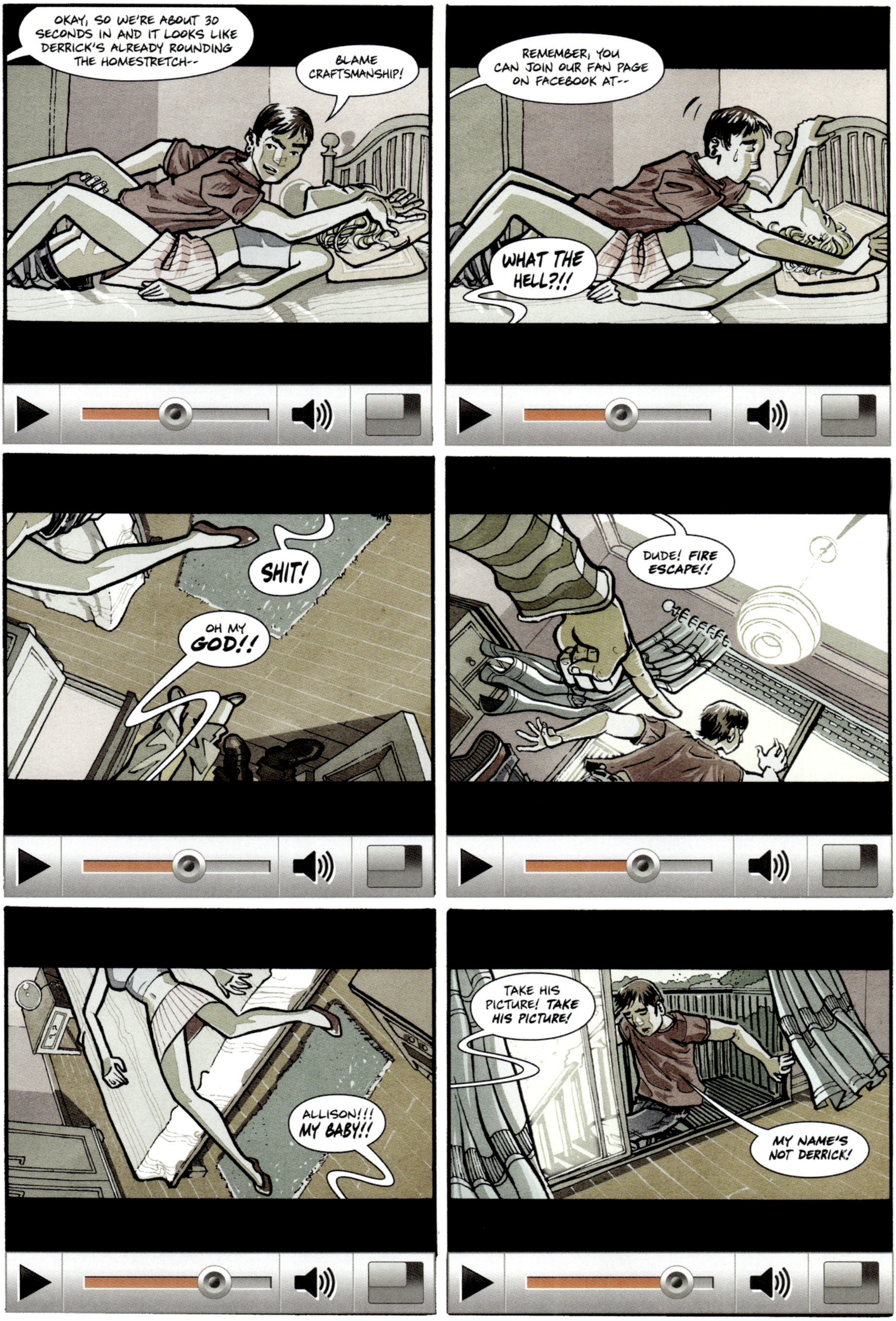
OKAY, SO WE'RE ABOUT 30 SECONDS IN AND IT LOOKS LIKE DERRICK'S ALREADY ROUNDING THE HOMESTRETCH--
BLAME CRAFTSMANSHIP!
REMEMBER, YOU CAN JOIN OUR FAN PAGE ON FACEBOOK AT--
WHAT THE HELL?!!
SHIT!
OH MY GOD!!
DUDE! FIRE ESCAPE!!
ALLISON!!! MY BABY!!
TAKE HIS PICTURE! TAKE HIS PICTURE!
MY NAME'S NOT DERRICK!

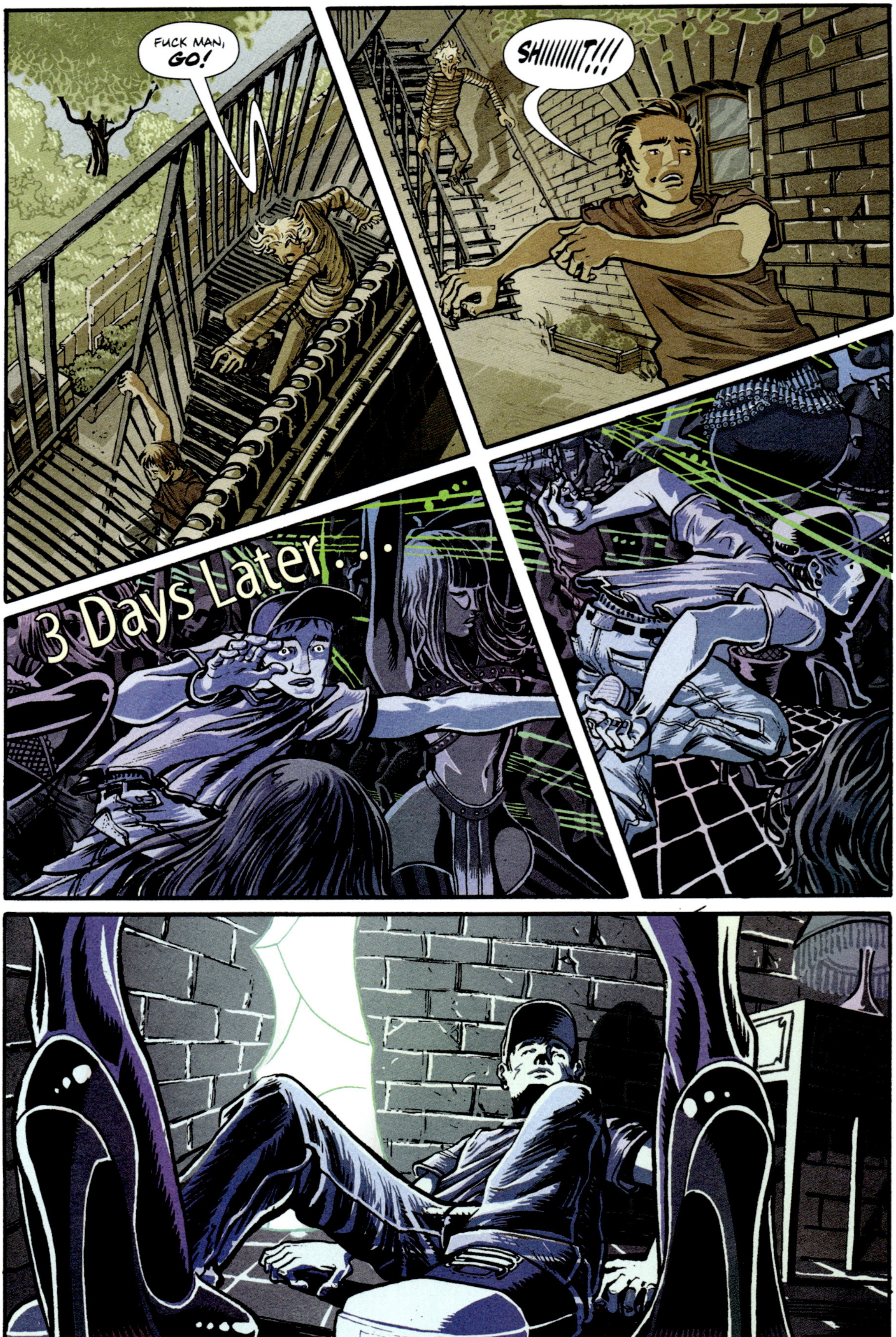
FUCK MAN, GO!
SHIIIIIIT!!!
3 Days Later...

BLAM!
OH MY GOD...
DO NOT ENTER
YOU SHOT HIM!
WHAT?
NO WAY, BITCH!
YOU DID.

OH FUCK!
YOU MEAN I--
--OH FUCK! I SHOT HIM! WHAT ARE WE GONNA DO?!!
'WHAT ARE WE GONNA DO, WHAT ARE WE GONNA DO?'
JESUS, LISTEN TO YOURSELF.
WE ARE GONNA TAKE THIS PRETTY LITTLE GUN THAT'S ALL NICE AND WARM NOW, AND GO FIND THAT STUPID FUCKER AND SHOOT HIM LIKE WE SHOULD'VE TEN MINUTES AGO.
THAT WAY JAMES WON'T CUT OUR CLITS OFF TOMORROW, GOT IT?
BUT--WHAT ABOUT HIM?
LEAVE HIM TO ME.

3 MONTHS EARLIER...
OKAY, SARA, VERY LOVELY, VERY LOVELY...
SoSoSara
So excited, doing a little film work today, director's supposedly coppolafied.
sent 2 minutes ago from Tweetie
NOW, WHAT I LIKE YOU TO DO IS BRUSH YOUR HAIR IN THE MIRROR, WHILE THE DOLL WATCHES, YES?
PERFECTO!
NOW, BRUSH THE DOLL'S HAIR, JUST SAME. LIKE IT IS YOU AGAIN, YES?
YES, YES... PERFECTO!
NOW, YOU ARE VERY TIRED, VERY SLEEPY...
...TIME FOR THE BEDDY-BED.
YOU AND DOLL ARE VERY TIRED.

PERFECTO!
YES, NOW YOU ARE VERY SLEEPY, DRIFTY DRIFTY...
NOW, TAKE DOLL, AND SHIT FUCK.
EXCUSE ME, I'M SORRY... IS THAT SOUTH AMERICAN FOR CUDDLING?
NO, NO... SHIT FUCK! YOU KNOW THE SHIT FUCKING, YES?
OKAY, THERE WAS THAT ONE TIME, BUT I WAS STUPID-DRUNK.
YES, SEE? SHE KNOWS THE SHIT FUCKING! SHE KNOWS! AMERICAN GIRLS ALL LOVE THE RUMPER!
UH HUH.
C'MERE.

AYYEE!
SoSoSara
Perfecto.
sent 8 seconds ago from Tweetie

HEY, YOU! WAIT!
WHAT, DID I FORGET TO SIGN A RELEASE OR SOMETHING?
THAT WAS PRETTY IMPRESSIVE BACK THERE. WHERE'D YOU LEARN TO HANDLE YOURSELF LIKE THAT?
I WENT TO AN ALL-BOYS SCHOOL.
WELL, IF YOU CAN GIVE ME ONE MINUTE, I HAVE A PROPOSITION FOR YOU--
SORRY, I'M NOT REALLY INTO BLACK GUYS.
YOU MISUNDERSTAND ME--
--I REPRESENT SOME VERY POWERFUL, VERY WELL-FINANCED INTERESTS--
YEAH, NOT INTO JEWISH GUYS EITHER.

JUST LISTEN.
THESE FILMS ARE A PART OF JUST ONE OF MANY VENTURES FOR US.
OUR BIGGEST REVENUE GENERATOR COMES FROM CONTRACTED DISMISSALS--USUALLY CORPORATE WHISTLEBLOWERS, CIVIL COURT PLAINTIFFS, INVESTIGATIVE JOURNALISTS...
...NOW, AS BUSINESS GROWS, WE'RE SEEING MORE JOBS INVOLVING HIGH-LEVEL, HARD-TO-REACH TARGETS.
I'M TALKING ABOUT PEOPLE WHO LIVE IN VERY EXCLUSIVE, VERY **PROTECTED** CIRCLES.
AND AS SECURITY TIGHTENS, IT'S GOTTEN HARDER TO INSERT PLANTS INTO THESE ENVIRONMENTS.
SO, I'VE GOT A PLAN ON MY EMPLOYER'S DESK, RIGHT NOW, TO TRIAL OUT TRAINING NEW AGENTS WHO DON'T **NEED** FALSIFIED CREDENTIALS. AGENTS WHO **ARE** WHAT THEY SAY THEY ARE.
HOUSEKEEPERS WHO ARE REGISTERED WITH A CLEANING SERVICE. REPAIRMEN WHO ARE D.O.B.-CERTIFIED. AND...NOW THIS ONE WE EXPECT TO BE GETTING A **LOT** OF USE OUT OF--
--MODELS WHO ARE LISTED AT ACTUAL AGENCIES. ONES WHO CAN GET INTO THE PARTIES AND FUNCTIONS WE CAN'T.
AND SOMEONE WITH YOUR OBVIOUS LEVEL OF AGGRESSION COULD BE--
WAIT... ARE YOU--ARE YOU ASKING ME TO BE A ***PROFESSIONAL KILLER?***
WELL... YES.
I WANNA MAKE OUT WITH YOU SO HARD RIGHT NOW.

3 MONTHS LATER...
ENTER
...AND THEN SHE ATE ALL MY PEANUT BUTTER OREOS!
I MEAN, WHAT KIND OF FRIEND DOES THAT, ANYWAY?
HEEEEELP ME...
DO NOT ENTER
SHE'S ALWAYS BEEN LIKE THIS. EVERYTHING'S ABOUT HER, ALL THE TIME.
SHE DOESN'T CARE ABOUT KILLING THAT GUY, SHE JUST CARES WHAT PEOPLE WILL THINK OF HER IF SHE DOES.
IT DRIVES ME NUTS!
YOU KNOW ANYONE LOOKING FOR A ROOMMATE?
ENTER
PLEASE, FOR GOD'S SAKE, CALL AN AMBULANCE, I'M--
CALL A WHAT?
AND GET ARRESTED FOR ANIMAL CRUELTY OR SOMETHING? NO WA--
--OOP, TEXT MESSAGE.
From: James
Status?
LOOK, I'M REALLY SORRY. WE SHOULDA PUT YOU OUT OF YOUR MISERY EARLIER. BUT SONIA'S GOT THE GUN RIGHT NOW, AND I FIND THE WHOLE STRANGULATION THING TO BE JUST WAY TOO EROTIC.
SO YOU'RE EITHER GONNA HAVE TO BE PATIENT HERE OR START MOVING TOWARD THE LIGHT.
Soon.

2 MONTHS EARLIER...
WELL, SARA, I HAVE TO GIVE YOU A LOT OF CREDIT.
EVERYONE WHO'S BEEN A PART OF YOUR TRAINING OVER THE LAST MONTH HAS BEEN SINGING YOUR PRAISES TO ME.
APPARENTLY, YOU'RE QUITE THE NATURAL.
BUT THIS-- THIS IS THE REAL TEST. THIS IS YOUR FIRST KILL.
IT ISN'T TARGET PRACTICE, OR SPARRING, THIS TIME IT COUNTS. THAT MAN SITTING OVER THERE IS ABOUT TO DIE, BECAUSE OF YOU. YOU ARE ABOUT TO TAKE A HUMAN LIFE.
NOW, I'VE BEEN IN YOUR SHOES HERE. I KNOW HOW DIFFERENT THIS IS, NO MATTER HOW MUCH YOU'VE TRIED TO MENTALLY PREPARE YOURSELF FOR IT.
I KNOW HOW HARD IT CAN BE TO LOOK INTO THEIR EYES JUST BEFORE.
YOU'RE PROBABLY STARTING TO THINK, 'DOES THIS GUY HAVE A WIFE? DOES HE HAVE KIDS? MAYBE HE'S--'
BLAM! BLAM! BLAM!
...JESUS.

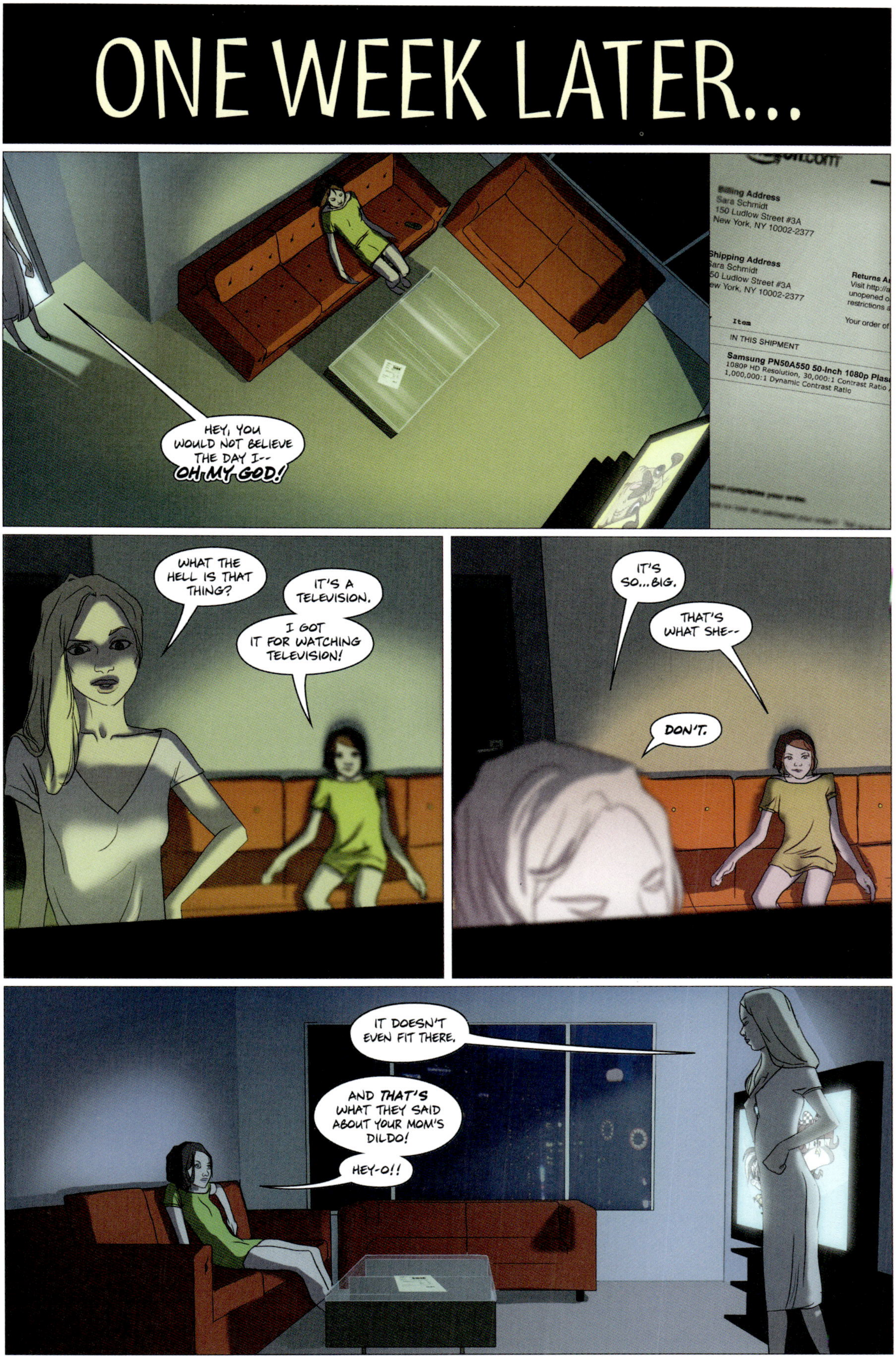
ONE WEEK LATER...
Billing Address
Sara Schmidt
150 Ludlow Street #3A
New York, NY 10002-2377
Shipping Address
Returns
Item
IN THIS SHIPMENT
1080P HD Resolution, 30,000:1 Contrast Ratio
1,000,000:1 Dynamic Contrast Ratio
HEY, YOU WOULD NOT BELIEVE THE DAY I-- OH MY GOD!
WHAT THE HELL IS THAT THING?
IT'S A TELEVISION.
I GOT IT FOR WATCHING TELEVISION!
IT'S SO...BIG.
THAT'S WHAT SHE--
DON'T.
IT DOESN'T EVEN FIT THERE.
AND THAT'S WHAT THEY SAID ABOUT YOUR MOM'S DILDO!
HEY-O!!

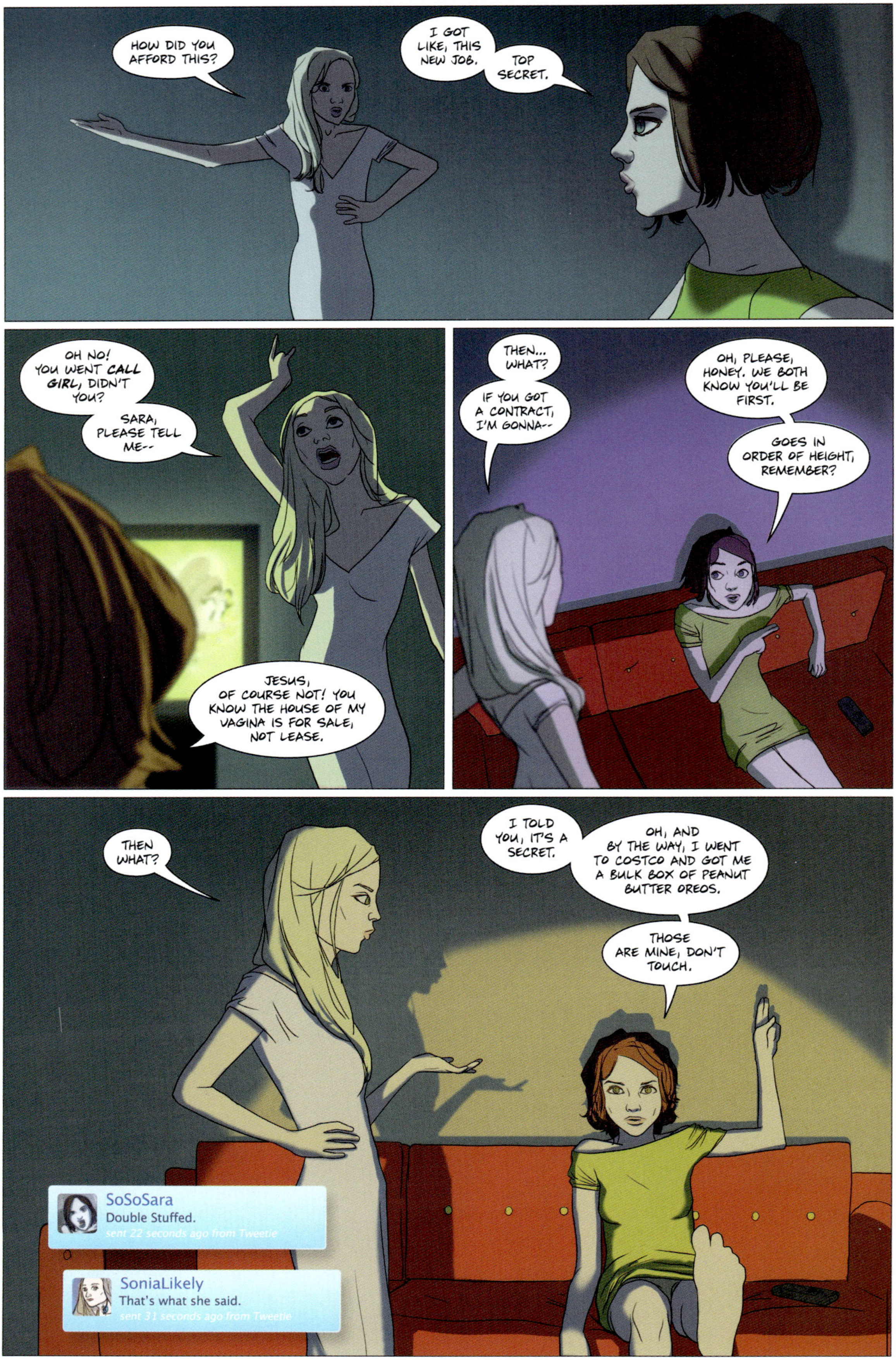
HOW DID YOU AFFORD THIS?
I GOT LIKE, THIS NEW JOB.
TOP SECRET.
OH NO! YOU WENT CALL GIRL, DIDN'T YOU?
SARA, PLEASE TELL ME--
JESUS, OF COURSE NOT! YOU KNOW THE HOUSE OF MY VAGINA IS FOR SALE, NOT LEASE.
THEN... WHAT?
IF YOU GOT A CONTRACT, I'M GONNA--
OH, PLEASE, HONEY. WE BOTH KNOW YOU'LL BE FIRST.
GOES IN ORDER OF HEIGHT, REMEMBER?
THEN WHAT?
I TOLD YOU, IT'S A SECRET.
OH, AND BY THE WAY, I WENT TO COSTCO AND GOT ME A BULK BOX OF PEANUT BUTTER OREOS.
THOSE ARE MINE, DON'T TOUCH.
SoSoSara
Double Stuffed.
sent 22 seconds ago from Tweetie
SoniaLikely
That's what she said.
sent 31 seconds ago from Tweetie

YOU DON'T EVEN WATCH TV.
BULLSHIT!
YOU KNOW I WATCH LARRY HOWARD EVERY NIGHT!
LIVE FROM ABN STUDIOS IN NEW YORK, IT'S TIME FOR **THE REALLY LATE SHOW**, WITH YOUR HOST--LARRY HOWARD!!
OH GOD, NOT THIS AGAIN.
AND NOW HE'S LIFE-SIZE, AND IN **HD.**
IF I CAN GET THIS REMOTE TO VIBRATE, I'M SET.
HOW'S EVERYBODY DOING TONIGHT?!!
THAT GUY'S MOVIES WERE TERRIBLE. WHY DID THEY GIVE HIM A TALK SHOW?
PROBABLY ALL THE LETTERS I SENT.
OZZIE TRAVERS AND THE REALLY LATE NIGHT BAND, LET'S HEAR IT FOR THEM! YEAH!
YOU'RE DERANGED.
WE'VE GOT A GREAT SHOW FOR YOU TONIGHT... ALLIE SIMONE IS HERE! YEAH, GIVE IT UP FOR ALLIE SIMONE-- AND OUR MUSICAL GUEST TONIGHT, LA ROUX! YEAH! BUT FIRST, I WAS WALKING DOWN FIFTH AVENUE TODAY--
WELL, HE'S ON NOW, SO YOU NEED TO GET THE FUCK OUT.
CAN'T HAVE YOU STANDING THERE SCOWLING WHILE I FINGER.
OR CAN I??!!

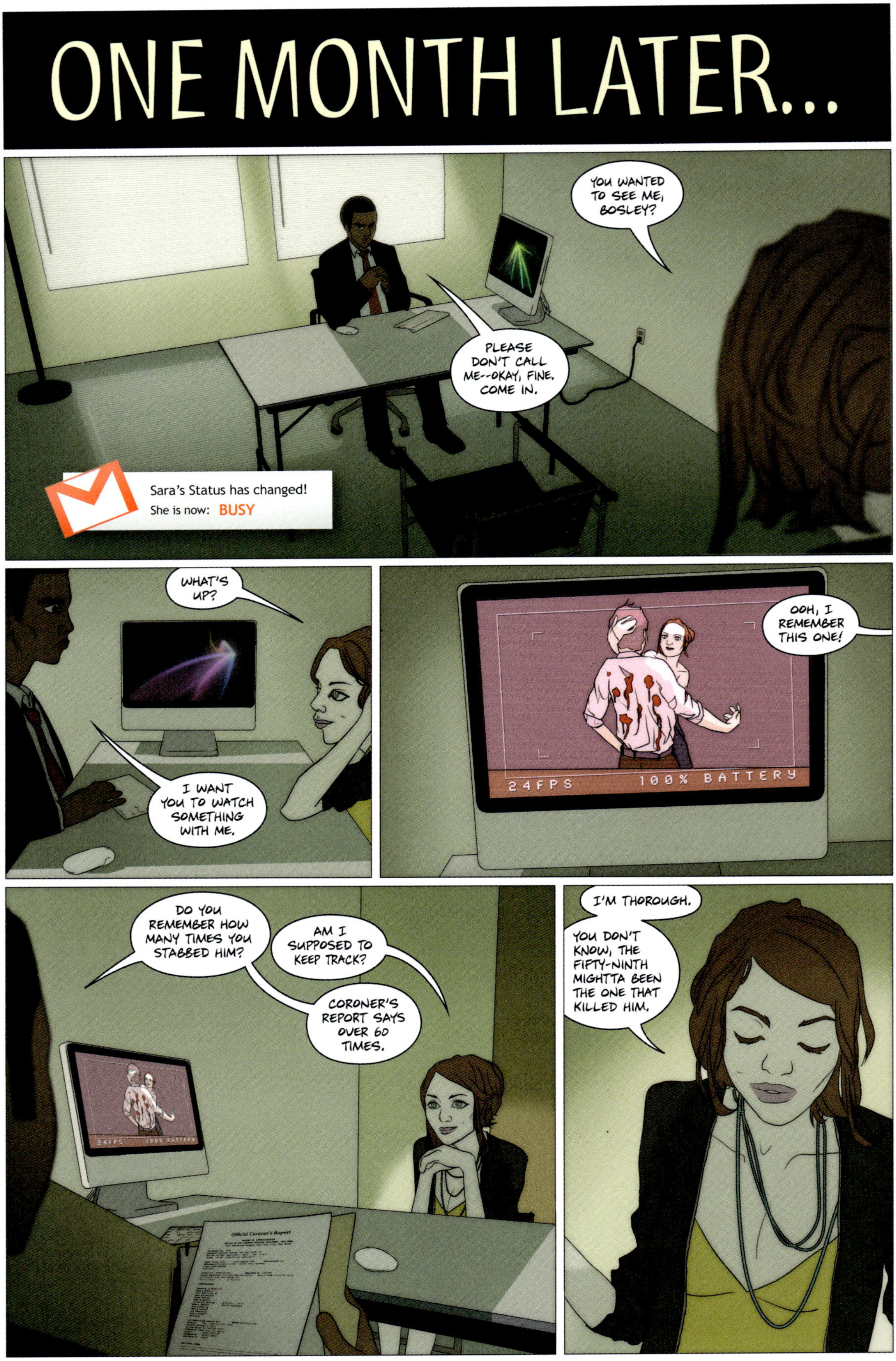
ONE MONTH LATER...
YOU WANTED TO SEE ME, BOSLEY?
PLEASE DON'T CALL ME--OKAY, FINE. COME IN.
Sara's Status has changed! She is now: BUSY
WHAT'S UP?
I WANT YOU TO WATCH SOMETHING WITH ME.
OOH, I REMEMBER THIS ONE!
24FPS 100% BATTERY
DO YOU REMEMBER HOW MANY TIMES YOU STABBED HIM?
AM I SUPPOSED TO KEEP TRACK?
CORONER'S REPORT SAYS OVER 60 TIMES.
Official Coroner's Report
I'M THOROUGH.
YOU DON'T KNOW, THE FIFTY-NINTH MIGHTTA BEEN THE ONE THAT KILLED HIM.

LOOK, SARA... DON'T GET ME WRONG. YOU'RE DOING EXCELLENT WORK. MY SUPERIORS ARE VERY PLEASED WITH YOUR PERFORMANCE.
WELL SEE, THERE THEN.
PEOPLE ARE DYING, EVERYONE'S MAKING MONEY, WHAT'S THE PROBLEM?
THE PROBLEM IS I'VE SEEN THIS BEFORE. YOU'RE LETTING YOUR EMOTIONS TAKE OVER.
IT'S CALLED PROFESSIONAL KILLING FOR A REASON.
I LOVE MY WORK, WHAT CAN I SAY?
I'M TELLING YOU THIS--YOU'VE GOT SOME DARK PLACES INSIDE YOU, AND YOU'RE GOING TO THE WELL TOO OFTEN.
I WATCH THIS TAPE, I SEE SOMEONE ON THE VERGE OF BURNING OUT FAST. SOMEONE IN A PRETTY FRAGILE STATE.
DID YOU JUST CALL ME EMO?
I'M SAYING, WE NEED TO LIGHTEN YOUR WORKLOAD. WE'RE OVERTAXING YOU. BUT FIRST, WE'RE GOING TO NEED TO FIND A NEW OPERATIVE TO PICK UP THE SLACK.
SO I FIGURED I'D ASK--YOU KNOW ANY GIRLS WHO MIGHT BE INTERESTED?
WELL...
...THERE'S MY ROOMMATE...

3 WEEKS LATER...
-cough-
AMBULANCE... PLEASE...
BOY, YOU SURE DO LOVE AMBULANCES.
PLEASE...I CAN...I CAN GET YOU MONEY...
I'M SORRY, MONEYSAYSWHAT?
I SWEAR, I CAN...I'M RICH... JUST CALL MY...
UGH, I CAN'T HEAR YOU WITH THAT STUPID MASK ON, HOLD UP...
I CAN GET YOU MONEY, I WON'T TELL ANYONE...

PLEASE... M-MY NAME IS LARRY HOWARD... I'M THE HOST OF THE REALLY LATE SHOW ON ABN...
PLEASE, JUST CALL MY MANAGER...

WELL SHITFUCK ME.

OH MY GOD--
--I'M SORRY... IT'S JUST...
...I CAN'T BELIEVE IT'S YOU!
I KNOW THIS IS GONNA SOUND WEIRD AND ALL, BUT--
BUT, LIKE--
APPLAUSE
I AM YOUR BIGGEST FAN.
OKAY, LARRY, WE'RE ON IN 5... 4... 3... 2...

AAAAND WE'RE BACK!
OUR FIRST GUEST TONIGHT--
WOO-HOOOO!
WHISTLE!
WOOT!
CLAP! CLAP! CLAP!
APPLAUSE
CLAP! CLAP!
CLAP! CLAP!
CLAP! CLAP! CLAP!
--OUR FIRST GUEST TONIGHT WAS JUST NAMED ONE OF THE MOST POWERFUL PEOPLE IN THE ENTERTAINMENT BUSINESS BY ENTERTAINMENT WEEKLY... HER NEW FILM THE PAISLEY PENNY MOVIE JUST OPENED AT NUMBER ONE AT THE BOX OFFICE, AND SHE'S CURRENTLY ON TOUR PROMOTING HER HIT RECORD, SONGS FOR MY FATHER.
PLEASE WELCOME...
...BETHANY MAYERS!
"WE NEED TO TALK, LARRY."

IT'S ABOUT ESMERALDA.
WHO?
DON'T PULL THAT SHIT.
ESMERALDA, YOUR ASSISTANT.
FORMER ASSISTANT, FRANK.
WELL, THAT'S THE FIRST THING.
WHY'D YOU FIRE HER?
SHE WAS STEALING OFFICE SUPPLIES.
READY?
SLICE 'EM!
REALLY. THAT'S IT?
WE'RE TALKING ABOUT A YEAR'S SUPPLY OF PAPERCLIPS HERE.
I ALMOST CALLED THE FBI. NO ONE IN THE OFFICE COULD ATTACH ANYTHING TO ANYTHING.

LOOK, I'M YOUR MANAGER, LARRY. I'M TRYING TO LOOK OUT FOR YOUR INTERESTS HERE.
BUT IF ALL YOU'RE GONNA DO IS FUCK AROUND WITH ME--
I DON'T KNOW WHAT YOU'RE TALKING ABOUT!
LISTEN, I FIRED THE GIRL BECAUSE SHE WAS VERY RUDE TO MY MOTHER ON THE PHONE.
THAT'S MY ONE RULE, WHAT DO YOU WANT ME TO SAY?
AGGGGH-HHH!!!!
SHE'S GOING TO TMZ.
YOU MEAN LIKE THE JAW THING?
YOU HAVEN'T BEEN FUNNY WITHOUT WRITERS IN YEARS.
STOP TRYING.
SHE'S GOING TO TMZ AND SHE'S GOT A LOT OF SHIT.
THANK YOU...
...THANK YOU...
...THANK YOU...
WHAT-- WHAT KIND OF SHIT?

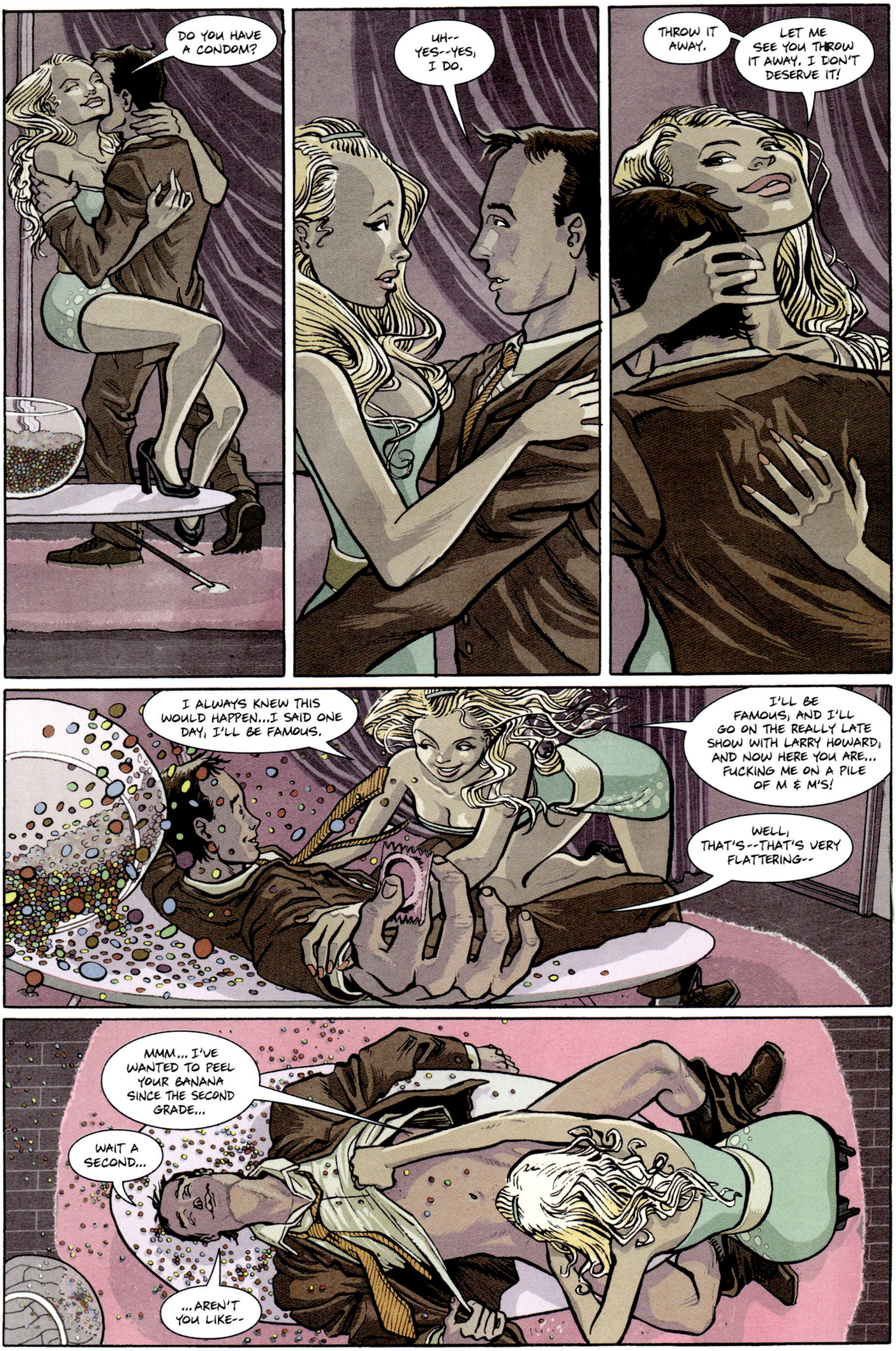
DO YOU HAVE A CONDOM?
UH-- YES--YES, I DO.
THROW IT AWAY.
LET ME SEE YOU THROW IT AWAY. I DON'T DESERVE IT!
I ALWAYS KNEW THIS WOULD HAPPEN...I SAID ONE DAY, I'LL BE FAMOUS.
I'LL BE FAMOUS, AND I'LL GO ON THE REALLY LATE SHOW WITH LARRY HOWARD, AND NOW HERE YOU ARE... FUCKING ME ON A PILE OF M & M'S!
WELL, THAT'S--THAT'S VERY FLATTERING--
MMM... I'VE WANTED TO PEEL YOUR BANANA SINCE THE SECOND GRADE...
WAIT A SECOND...
...AREN'T YOU LIKE--

FIFTEEN!
SHE'S FIFTEEN, LARRY! BETHANY MAYERS IS FIFTEEN.
I FORGOT!
REALLY? YOU **FORGOT** THAT THE MOST FAMOUS TEENAGER IN THE WORLD IS A TEENAGER?
WHAT, YOU KNOW HOW IT IS, THESE KIDS LOOK THIRTEEN UNTIL THEY'RE TWENTY SEVEN, IT'S IN THEIR CONTRACTS!
I'M NOT A **DOCTOR**--I DIDN'T EVEN HAVE MY CONTACTS IN!
DISNEY WANTED TO HAVE YOU KILLED, YOU KNOW THAT?
VERY FUNNY.
I'M NOT KIDDING.
THEY CUT YOUR BRAKES WHILE YOU WERE FILMING IN LA.
I HAD TO GET A REPAIRMAN OUT THERE IN THE MIDDLE OF THE NIGHT.
YOU'RE SERIOUS?
DON'T WORRY, I GOT YOU OUT OF IT.
YOU'RE GONNA HAVE TO DO SOME TIME AS THE VOICE OF A SKATEBOARDING **FERRET**, BUT YOU'LL LIVE.

THAT'S NOT THE WORST PART OF IT.
OF COURSE NOT, THAT'S NO BIG DEAL, RIGHT?
I MEAN-- THAT GIRL'S DONE A LOT OF TALK SHOWS.
LARRY, I NEED YOU TO BE HONEST WITH ME HERE.
WHAT CAN YOU TELL ME--
ABOUT THE SUIT?

WHAT, THIS? IT'S HUGO BOSS. WHY, YOU NEED A TAILOR?
MY GUY DOESN'T DO BIG AND TALL, I DON'T THINK.
OKAY, FUCK THIS--
YOU DON'T WANNA PLAY BALL? THEY'RE GONNA RUN THIS SHIT IN THE NEXT 24 HOURS. YOUR CAREER IS OVER, YOU UNDERSTAND? I'M NOT GONNA--
FRANK, WAIT.
WAIT...
... JUST... GIVE ME A SECOND.
WHAT CAN YOU TELL ME ABOUT THE SUIT, LARRY?
OKAY, OKAY...
...JUST...
WHAT CAN YOU TELL ME ABOUT THE SUIT?
OKAY. FINE. HERE IT IS.
I'VE BEEN--
--I'VE BEEN--
--I'VE BEEN MESSING AROUND ON THE CRAIG'S LIST.

Who wants some big love?

Date: 2009-11-04, 3:02AM EST

Reply To This Post

I got more ass than you need. You like food fun? My fridge is stocked!

Everywhere With Helicopter.

Date: 2009-06-21, 11:24PM EST

Reply To This Post

Some hot times with less getting in the way. Spin me round, flip me over, we can do it all.

Me, You, Spaghetti Dinner.

Date: 2008-12-09, 4:13AM EST

Reply To This Post

Exactly what it sounds like.

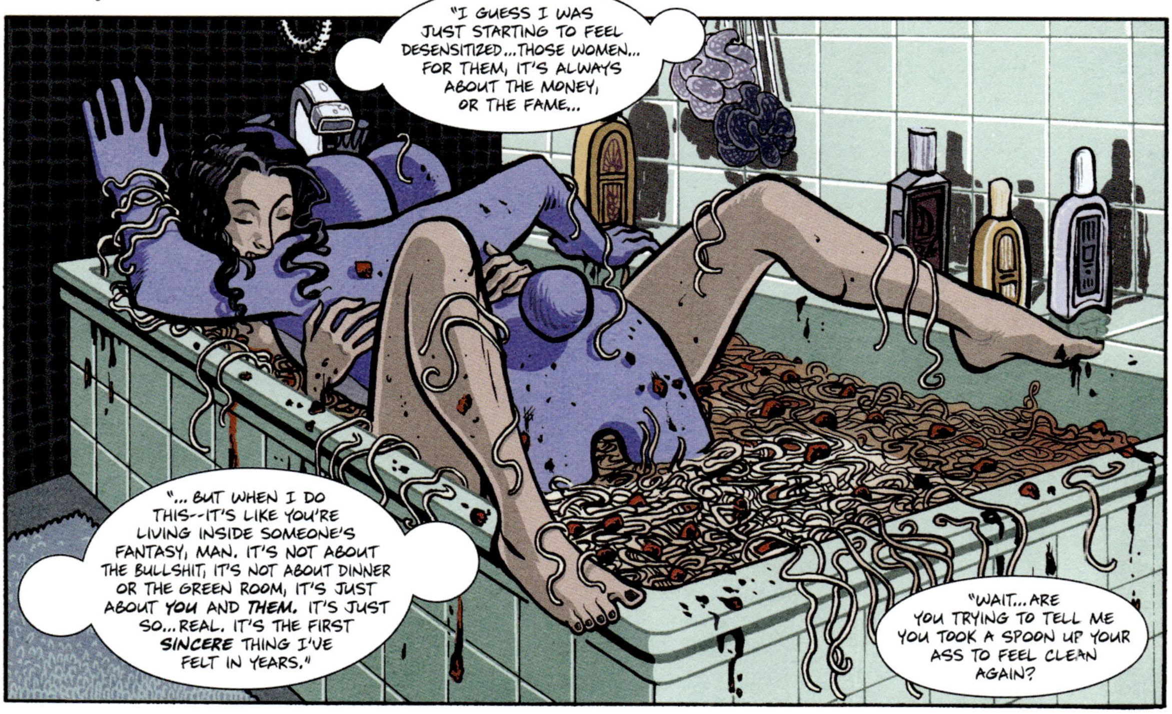

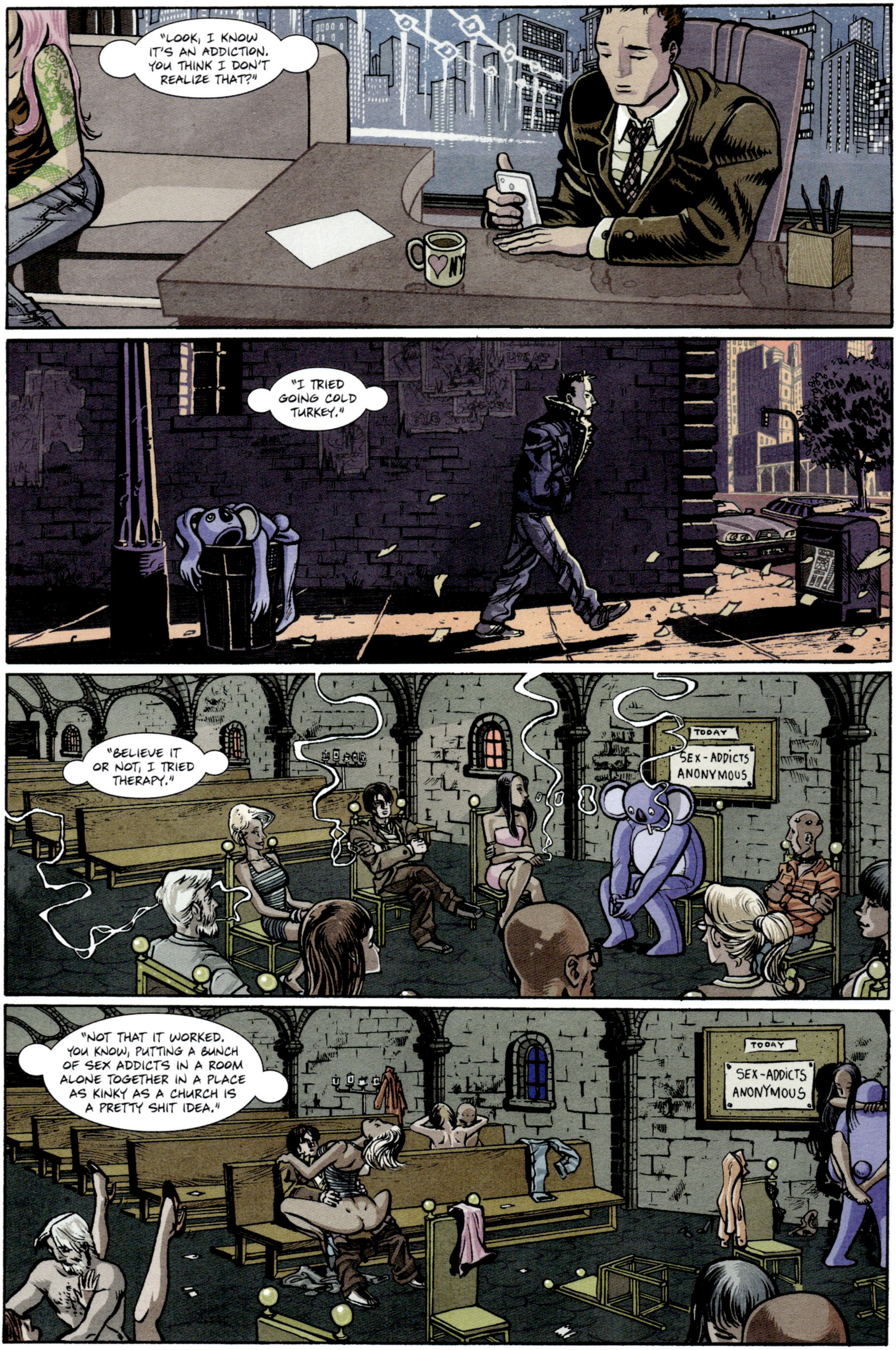
"LOOK, I KNOW IT'S AN ADDICTION. YOU THINK I DON'T REALIZE THAT?"
"I TRIED GOING COLD TURKEY."
"BELIEVE IT OR NOT, I TRIED THERAPY."
TODAY
SEX-ADDICTS ANONYMOUS
"NOT THAT IT WORKED. YOU KNOW, PUTTING A BUNCH OF SEX ADDICTS IN A ROOM ALONE TOGETHER IN A PLACE AS KINKY AS A CHURCH IS A PRETTY SHIT IDEA."
TODAY
SEX-ADDICTS ANONYMOUS

Dog Lovers Only!

Date: 2009-07-18, 8:33PM EST

Reply To This Post

Admit it, you've always been curious. come enjoy a unique, sensual performance that blends human, beast, and nature into a singular, beautiful moment of pure bliss. You won't believe your eyes. Email for address and password. No cameras or recording equipment allowed!

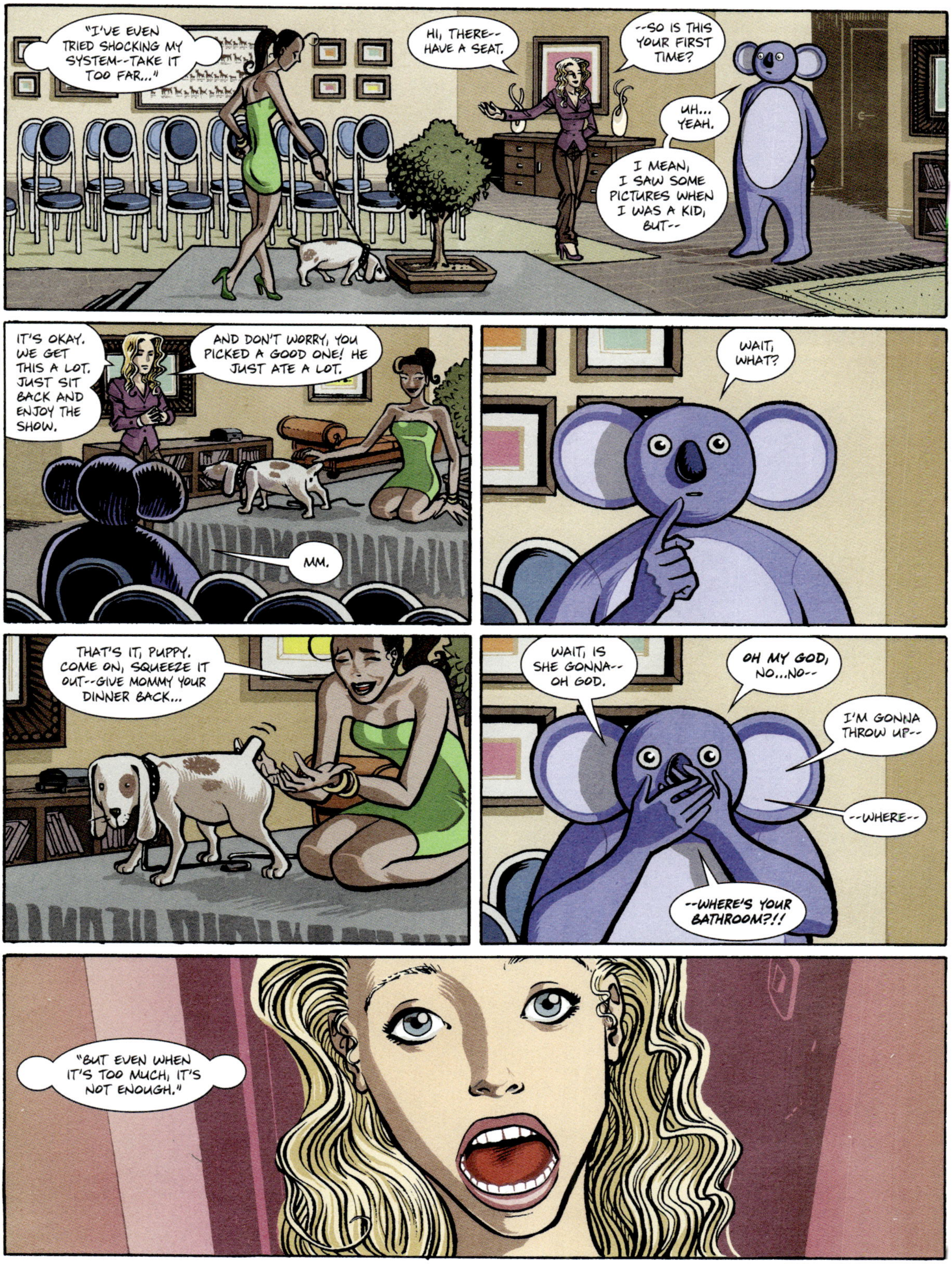

JESUS.
HOW BAD?
CHARLIE SHEEN. HUGH GRANT. EDDIE MURPHY. THAT KIND OF BAD.
AND YOU'VE BEEN EARNING A LIVING MAKING JOKES ABOUT OTHER PEOPLE DOING THIS SHIT, SO NOBODY'S GONNA SHOW YOU ANY MERCY.
WE'RE GONNA GET YOU CHECKED INTO A CLINIC. YOU'RE GONNA BE TALKING TO OPRAH...REGULARLY, START STUDYING UP ON YOUR VAGINASPEAK.
MIGHT BE ENOUGH TO SAVE THE LATE NIGHT GIG.
YOU CAN RULE OUT THE MOVIES FOR A WHILE, THOUGH.
BUT LARRY--
--SAVING THE JOB'S ONE THING. THAT'S EASY.
YOU NEED TO BE READY FOR WHAT LIFE'S GONNA BE LIKE IN 24 HOURS.
KNOW THAT DREAM WHERE YOU'RE STANDING IN FRONT OF A BIG AUDIENCE NAKED?
WELL, IT'S ABOUT TO COME TRUE.
MY ADVICE? TAKE TONIGHT, GET YOUR HEAD STRAIGHT.
BECAUSE TOMORROW, EVERYTHING YOU NEVER WANTED ANYBODY TO KNOW, WELL...EVERYBODY'S GONNA KNOW.
sigh
NO MATTER HOW LONG I DO THIS, I'LL NEVER GET YOU ASSHOLES.
I GREW UP IN PITTSBURGH. WHERE I'M FROM, LIFE STOPS BEATING THE SHIT OUT OF YOU, YOU SAY THANKS AND HOPE IT LASTS FOR A SECOND.
YOU PEOPLE--YOU GET EVERYTHING, AND YOU JUST CAN'T WAIT TO PISS IT ALL DOWN SOME WHORE'S MOUTH.

Cuckolding In The Club

Date: 2009-03-07, 2:15AM EST

Reply To This Post

You meet me in the back room at Forgetless tonight and take me while my boyfriend watches. If you need directions, let me know. Send pics and we'll set up a time.

P.S. Must be willing to let my boyfriend attack, injure, and/or physically violate you afterwards.

SLAM

LIVE FROM ABN STUDIOS IN NEW YORK!!! IT'S--
BLAM

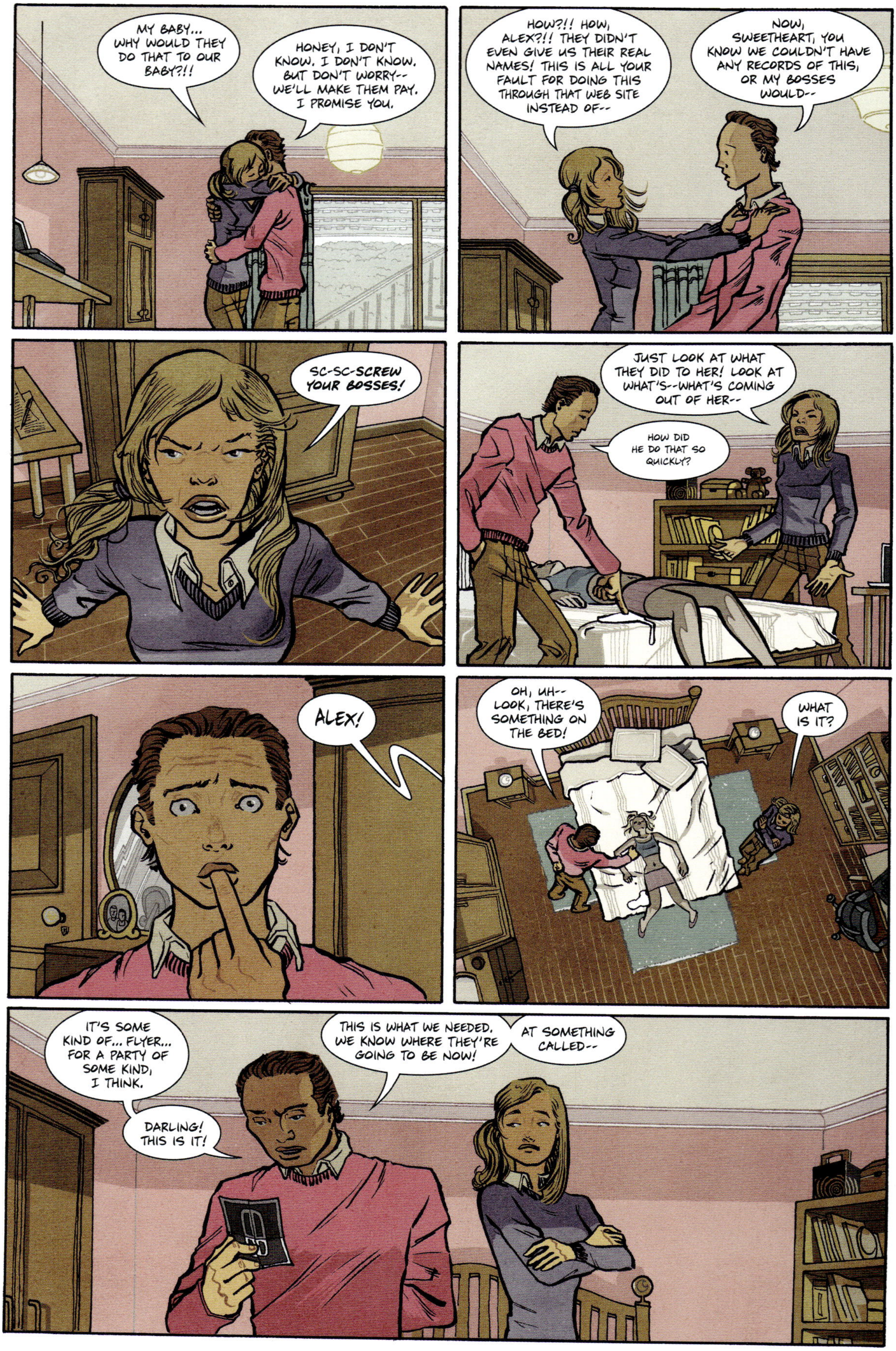
MY BABY... WHY WOULD THEY DO THAT TO OUR BABY?!!
HONEY, I DON'T KNOW. I DON'T KNOW. BUT DON'T WORRY-- WE'LL MAKE THEM PAY. I PROMISE YOU.
HOW?!! HOW, ALEX?!! THEY DIDN'T EVEN GIVE US THEIR REAL NAMES! THIS IS ALL YOUR FAULT FOR DOING THIS THROUGH THAT WEB SITE INSTEAD OF--
NOW, SWEETHEART, YOU KNOW WE COULDN'T HAVE ANY RECORDS OF THIS, OR MY BOSSES WOULD--
SC-SC-SCREW YOUR BOSSES!
JUST LOOK AT WHAT THEY DID TO HER! LOOK AT WHAT'S--WHAT'S COMING OUT OF HER--
HOW DID HE DO THAT SO QUICKLY?
ALEX!
OH, UH-- LOOK, THERE'S SOMETHING ON THE BED!
WHAT IS IT?
IT'S SOME KIND OF... FLYER... FOR A PARTY OF SOME KIND, I THINK.
DARLING! THIS IS IT!
THIS IS WHAT WE NEEDED. WE KNOW WHERE THEY'RE GOING TO BE NOW!
AT SOMETHING CALLED--

3 DAYS LATER...
UGH.
WHAT A DISASTER. LOOK AT THESE PEOPLE. I'D RATHER FUCK MY MOM THAN MOST OF THESE GUYS.
DON'T TELL THEM THAT, THEY'LL THINK YOU'RE FLIRTING.
DO I GET SOME KIND OF PARTIAL PAYMENT IF THIS GUY DOESN'T SHOW? BECAUSE AN HOUR OF LOOKING, ALL THESE BROOKLYN VEGAN READERS ARE STARTING TO LOOK ALIKE TO ME.
JUST GO GET ANOTHER DRINK, I'LL KEEP LOOKING.
AND DON'T GIVE UP, LIL' SWIMMER, WE'LL FIND HIM. ANY LUCK, THIS GUY WILL BE DEAD BEFORE LAST CALL.

I AM GONNA LIVE FOREVER!!!
JESUS, HOW MUCH ADDERALL DID YOU TAKE?
NOT ENOUGH TO STOP THIS MAGICAL BONER!
OH, COME ON, MAN...LOOK AT THIS--IT'S THE FINAL FORGETLESS!
WE'RE A PART OF NEW YORK HISTORY NOW. THE BIGGEST PARTY OF THE YEAR, THE DECADE, THE CENTURY...AND WE JUST WALKED IN THE DOOR.
PEOPLE ARE GONNA BE TALKING ABOUT THIS FOR A LONG DAMN TIME, DUDE.
YEAH, FEELS JUST LIKE THE MOON LANDING OR SOMETHING.
LOOKS JUST LIKE THE LAST LAST FORGETLESS FAR AS I CAN TELL.
NOW, IF YOU'LL EXCUSE ME, I'M GONNA GO FIND A GIRL TO GIVE THIS HERPES TO.
HEY THERE.

I'M JASON.
I'M MENSTRUATING.
YEAH, NOT GONNA LET THAT STOP ME.
SO WHAT BRINGS YOU OUT HERE TONIGHT?
ME?
I'M HERE TO KILL SOMEONE.
REALLY? 'CAUSE I COULD RECOMMEND ABOUT HALF THE CROWD HERE. WE CAN START WITH THE GIRLS WHO HAVE ALREADY TURNED ME DOWN--
OKAY--LOOK, BUSHWICK--
--I APPRECIATE YOUR WHOLE 'DARE TO DREAM' ATTITUDE, IT'S VERY INSPIRING, BUT REALLY, I'VE GOT A LOT ON MY MIND RIGHT NOW--
WELL, NOW, THAT RIGHT THERE SOUNDS LIKE A PROBLEM. MAYBE I CAN HELP.
...
NO, REALLY!
I'M A HYPNOTIST.
UNLESS MY PROBLEM IS FAILING TO GET THE ENTERTAINMENT FOR MY PARENTS' ANNIVERSARY PARTY, I'M NOT EXACTLY SURE HOW THAT'S SUPPOSED TO HELP ME.
FINE. LET ME SHOW YOU.

OKAY... JUST... CLEAR YOUR MIND... LET ALL YOUR THOUGHTS FADE AWAY... FADE AWAY...
NOW...FOCUS ON THE WATCH. BACK AND FORTH...BACK AND FORTH...
GOOD. NOW... WHEN I CLAP MY HANDS, YOU WILL FORGET ALL YOUR PROBLEMS AND FALL IN LOVE WITH THE NEXT GUY YOU SEE...
SONIA!

20 MINUTES LATER...
DO NOT
ENTER
BLAM!!!

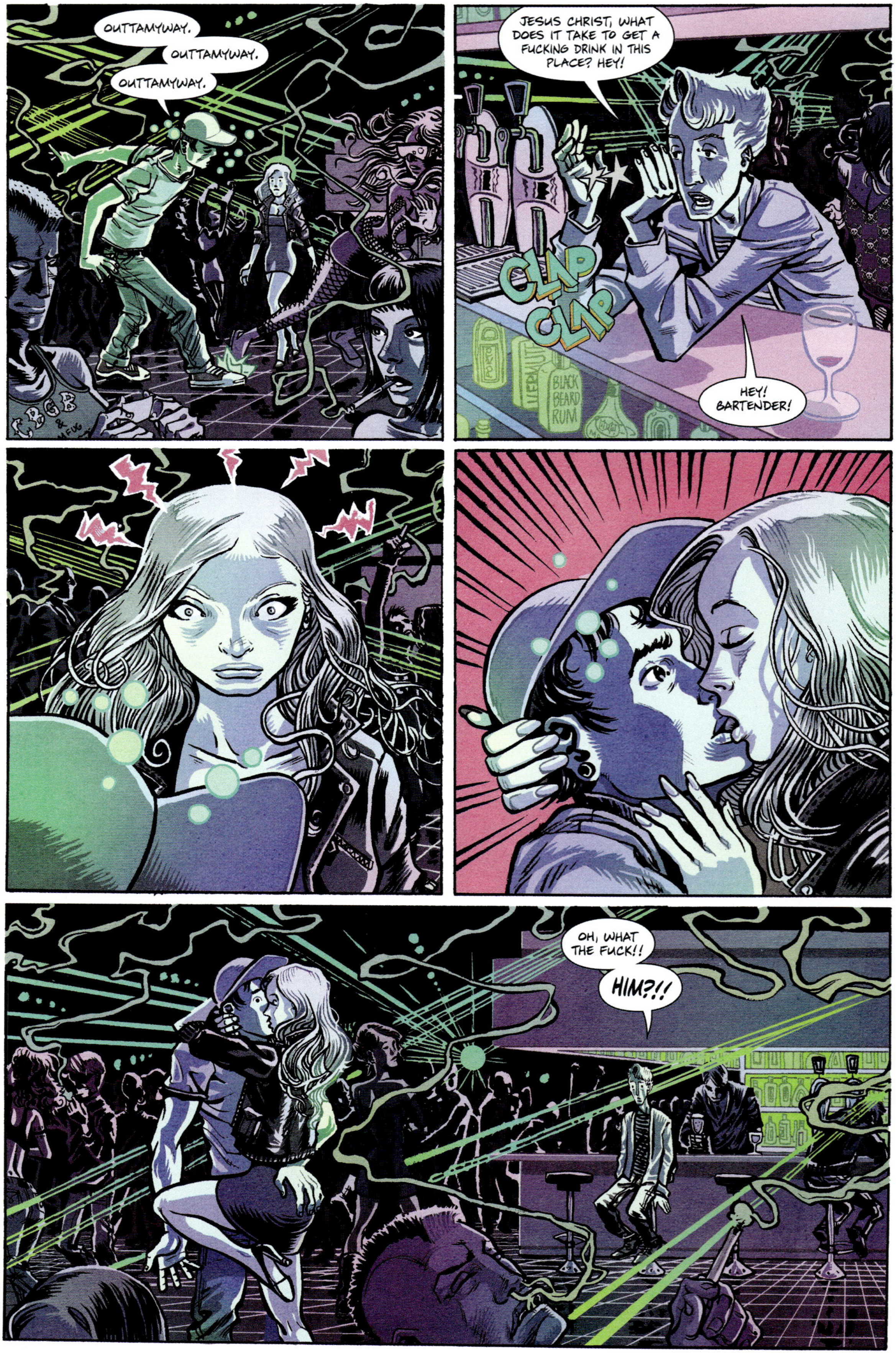
OUTTAMYWAY.
OUTTAMYWAY.
OUTTAMYWAY.
CBGB
JESUS CHRIST, WHAT DOES IT TAKE TO GET A FUCKING DRINK IN THIS PLACE? HEY!
CLAP
CLAP
BLACK BEARD RUM
HEY! BARTENDER!
OH, WHAT THE FUCK!!
HIM?!!

10 MINUTES LATER...
OH GOD... WAKE UP, PLEASE WAKE UP... DON'T DIE WITHOUT AN ERECTION, PLEASE...
ARE YOU... ≶COUGH≷ REALLY A FAN?
OH JESUS, YEAH! YOU'VE GOT NO IDEA.
YOU'RE THE ENTIRE REASON I PREFER SEX ON DESKS.
THEN... YOU WON'T LET ME DIE?
LET YOU-- OH FUCK NO!
WE ARE GONNA GET YOU TO A HOSPITAL RIGHT NOW!
DON'T WORRY, TU'S LARRY HOWARD, I'LL SAVE YOU!

I'M SERIOUS... YOU LOOK REALLY, REALLY FAMILIAR.
AH SCREW IT, WHO CARES.
YOU KNOW, I'VE NEVER REALLY DONE ANYTHING LIKE THIS BEFORE. I MEAN, I DON'T EVEN KNOW YOUR NAME.
THEY CALL ME SERPENTOR, BABY.
HAHA, YOU'RE FUNNY! LET'S--
OH MY GOD...

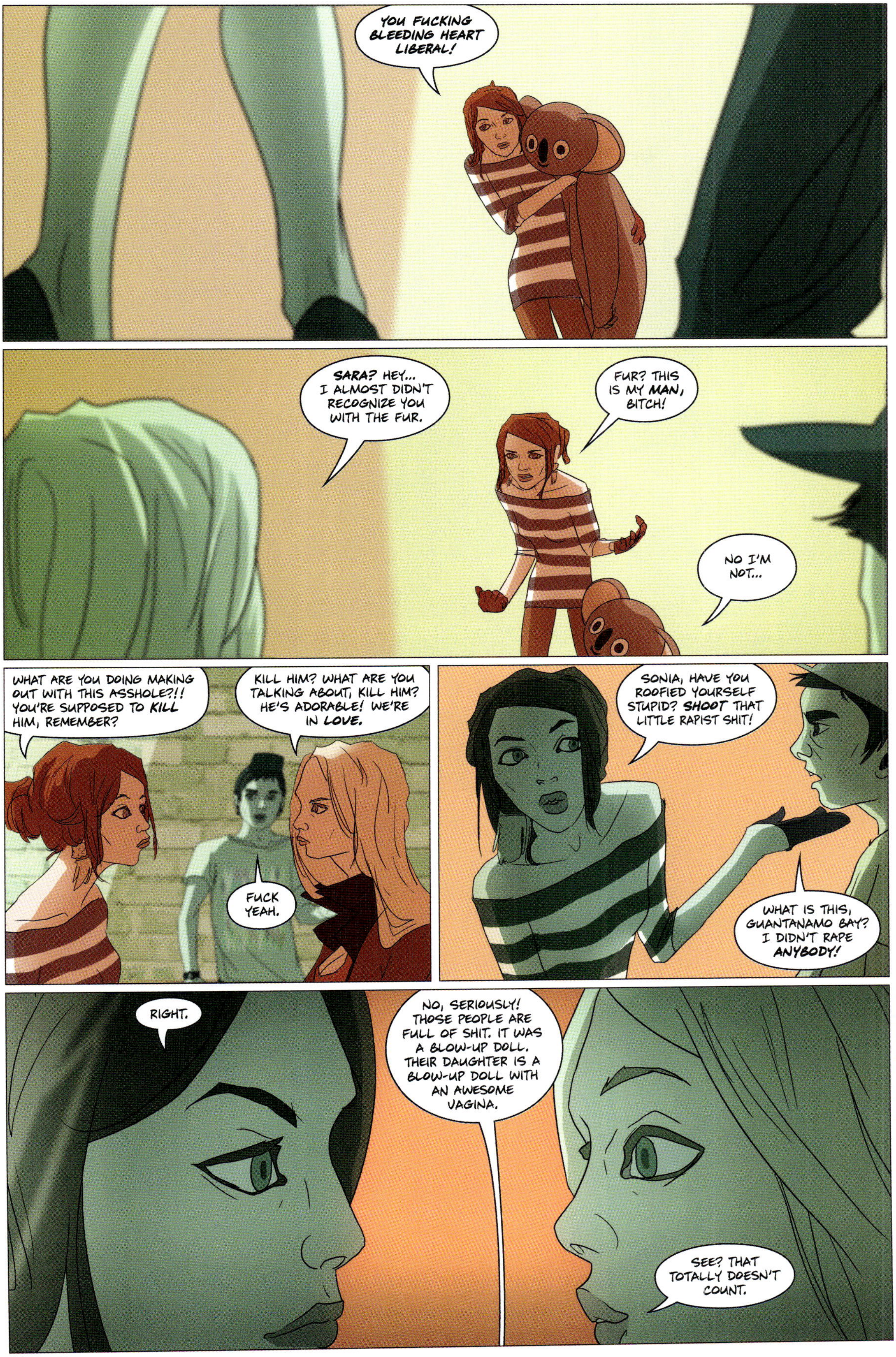
YOU FUCKING BLEEDING HEART LIBERAL!
SARA? HEY... I ALMOST DIDN'T RECOGNIZE YOU WITH THE FUR.
FUR? THIS IS MY MAN, BITCH!
NO I'M NOT...
WHAT ARE YOU DOING MAKING OUT WITH THIS ASSHOLE?!! YOU'RE SUPPOSED TO KILL HIM, REMEMBER?
KILL HIM? WHAT ARE YOU TALKING ABOUT, KILL HIM? HE'S ADORABLE! WE'RE IN LOVE.
FUCK YEAH.
SONIA, HAVE YOU ROOFIED YOURSELF STUPID? SHOOT THAT LITTLE RAPIST SHIT!
WHAT IS THIS, GUANTANAMO BAY? I DIDN'T RAPE ANYBODY!
RIGHT.
NO, SERIOUSLY! THOSE PEOPLE ARE FULL OF SHIT. IT WAS A BLOW-UP DOLL. THEIR DAUGHTER IS A BLOW-UP DOLL WITH AN AWESOME VAGINA.
SEE? THAT TOTALLY DOESN'T COUNT.

WHATEVER.
YOU THINK JAMES GIVES A FUCK ABOUT THIS GUY'S PENETRATION SITUATION? BOTTOM LINE, SOMEBODY PAID GOOD MONEY FOR THIS DUDE TO GET IT.
KRRSHHH
AND HELL, I WANNA KILL HIM JUST FOR APPEARANCE'S SAKE.
BACK OFF, SARA.
SERIOUSLY?
I SHOULDA SEEN THIS COMING.
FIRST THE OREOS, NOW THIS.
YOU'RE A FUCKING PSYCHO. YOU'RE LIKE A SERIAL KILLER, YOU KNOW THAT? I HEAR THOSE GUYS CAN'T PULL OFF ORGASMS EITHER.
YOU SHOOT ME, I AM GONNA NEO THAT BULLET RIGHT BACK AT YOU, YOU FUCKING CUNT.
BLAM!!!

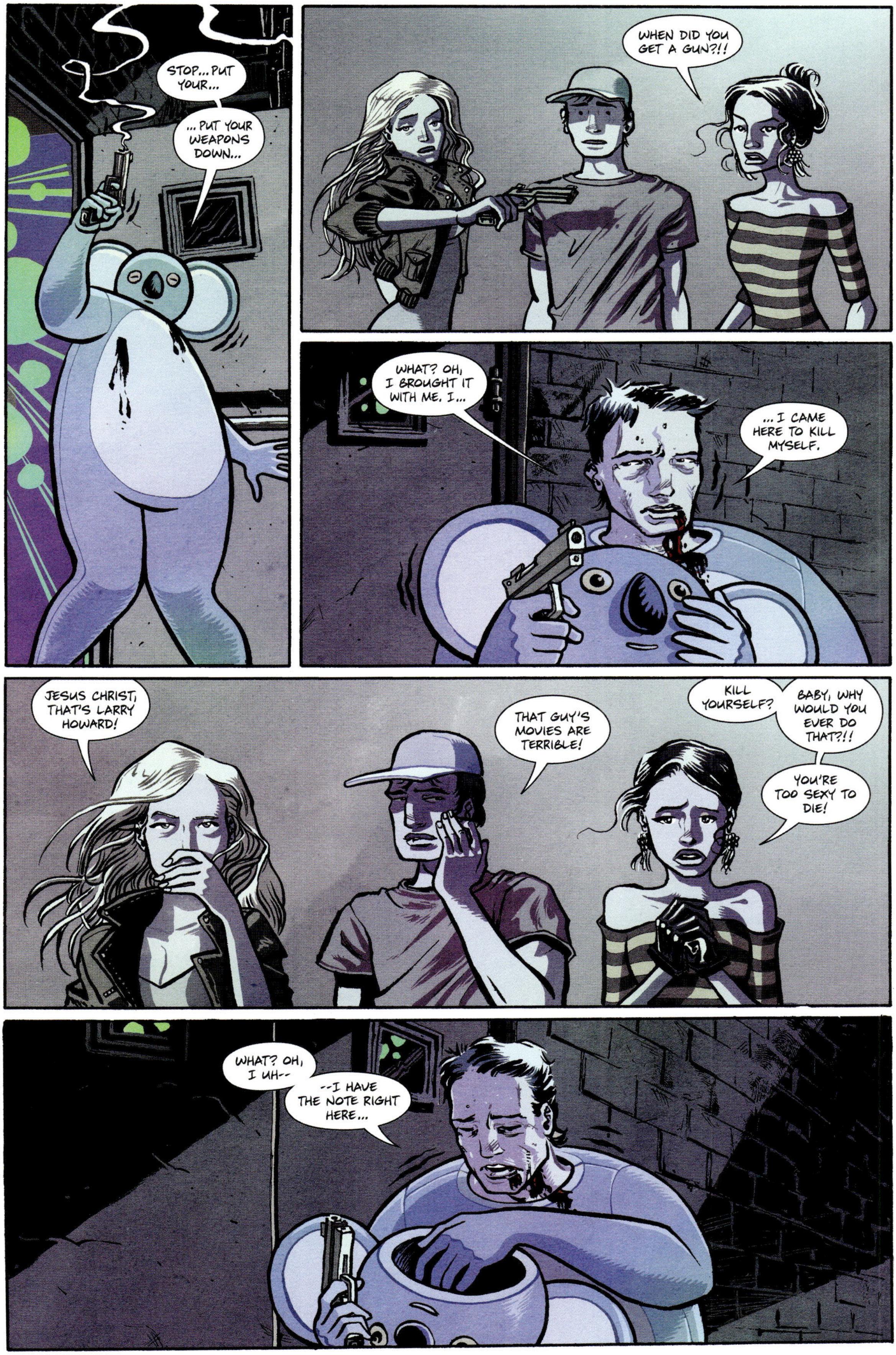
STOP... PUT YOUR...
... PUT YOUR WEAPONS DOWN...
WHEN DID YOU GET A GUN?!!
WHAT? OH, I BROUGHT IT WITH ME. I...
... I CAME HERE TO KILL MYSELF.
JESUS CHRIST, THAT'S LARRY HOWARD!
THAT GUY'S MOVIES ARE TERRIBLE!
KILL YOURSELF?
BABY, WHY WOULD YOU EVER DO THAT?!!
YOU'RE TOO SEXY TO DIE!
WHAT? OH, I UH--
--I HAVE THE NOTE RIGHT HERE...

DAMN IT, I CAN'T READ THIS... EVERYTHING'S A LITTLE BLURRY, YOU KNOW?
I GUESS WHAT IT ALL COMES DOWN TO IS I, UH... I REALLY HATE NEW YORK.
I MEAN, WHEN I FIRST GOT HERE, ALL I REALLY WANTED TO DO WAS GET FAMOUS, GET RICH...JUST MAKE EVERYBODY NOTICE HOW SPECIAL I WAS. ALL I REALLY WANTED WAS FOR PEOPLE TO NOTICE ME.
BUT AFTER A WHILE, IT JUST STARTS MAKING YOU DO ALL THESE THINGS YOU DON'T WANT TO DO...JUST SO YOU CAN SURVIVE.
SO I SAID YEAH, SURE, I CAN DO THAT. BUT I NEVER REALLY WANTED TO, YOU KNOW?
AND IT ALL JUST...IT JUST CHANGES YOU, I GUESS. ALL THAT'S LEFT ARE THE WORST PARTS OF YOURSELF.
YOU START DOING THESE AWFUL, HORRIBLE THINGS JUST TO PROVE TO YOURSELF THAT YOU BELONG HERE.
DOES THAT MAKE SENSE?
...YEAH. YEAH IT DOES.
JESUS, SONIA, I CAN'T BELIEVE YOU SHOT MY DREAM GUY!
NO...SHE DIDN'T.

30 MINUTES EARLIER (OR SOMETHING LIKE THAT)...
YOU LITTLE FUCKER! I AM GONNA--
BLAM
BLAM

30 MINUTES LATER...
SO...I DIDN'T KILL HIM?
WELL, YOU ARE A PISS-POOR SHOT.
WHY WOULD YOU SHOOT YOURSELF IN THE CHEST?!!
HUH? OH...CELEBRITY FUNERAL. PEOPLE ARE GONNA WANT TO TAKE PICTURES.
BUT...IF YOU HAD A GUN, YOU COULD'VE JUST KILLED ME WHEN WE WERE WAITING BACK THERE--
WHAT?
I COULDN'T KILL ANYBODY...I'M A COMEDIAN...
BUT, PLEASE, GUYS...I DON'T WANNA DIE ANYMORE...
...PLEASE... CAN SOMEBODY TAKE ME TO A HOSPITAL NOW? I-- OHHHHHH...
WELL?!! ARE YOU TWO GONNA HELP ME OR WHAT?!!

30 MINUTES LATER...
I GUESS WE DID THE RIGHT THING, YEAH?
GUESS SO, MOOKIE.
JAMES IS GONNA BE PRETTY PISSED ABOUT US NOT KILLING DERRICK, THOUGH.
NAH, HE TEXTED ME AND CANCELED THE HIT WHILE WE WERE IN THE AMBULANCE.
REALLY?
Messages
James
May 3, 2009 4:36 AM
Turns out the contract's just had all his assets seized by the feds. He's been running some kind of gay porn piracy...
... web site for the last six months. No money, no kill. Sonia can call it a night. How'd she do btw?
Who, Sonia? Stone Cold Killer.
OH, I GOT YOU THESE.
AW DANG, PEANUT BUTTER OREOS! MY *BABIES!*
I STILL OWE YOU A FEW HUNDRED OF THEM, I GUESS.
WELL, IT'S A START, ROOMIE-LOVE. AND HEY, LOOK AT IT THIS WAY--WE *BOTH* MET GUYS TONIGHT! FORGETLESS FINALLY COMES THROUGH!
YEAH... I GUESS--

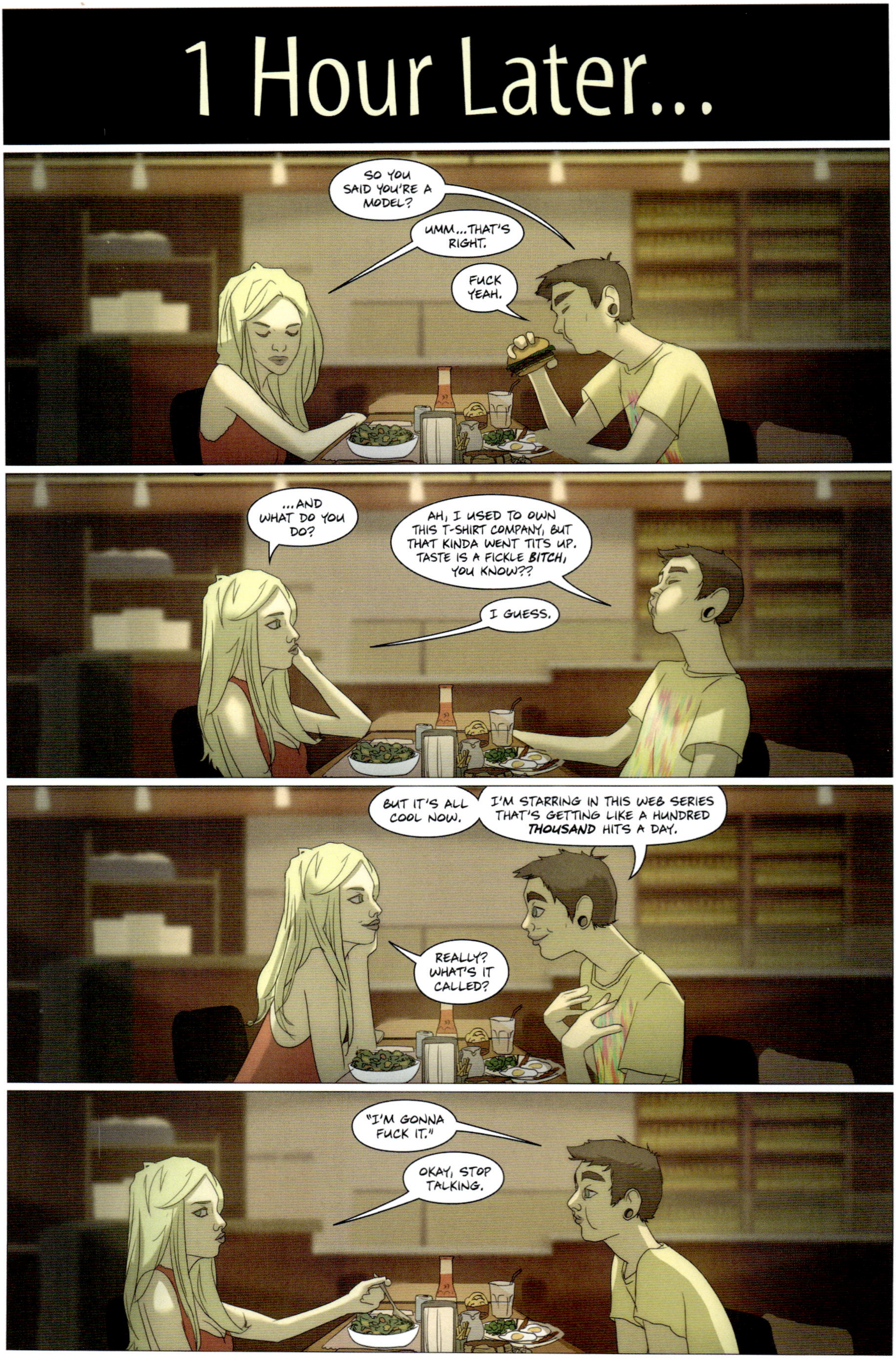
1 Hour Later...
SO YOU SAID YOU'RE A MODEL?
UMM...THAT'S RIGHT.
FUCK YEAH.
...AND WHAT DO YOU DO?
AH, I USED TO OWN THIS T-SHIRT COMPANY, BUT THAT KINDA WENT TITS UP. TASTE IS A FICKLE BITCH, YOU KNOW??
I GUESS.
BUT IT'S ALL COOL NOW.
I'M STARRING IN THIS WEB SERIES THAT'S GETTING LIKE A HUNDRED THOUSAND HITS A DAY.
REALLY? WHAT'S IT CALLED?
"I'M GONNA FUCK IT."
OKAY, STOP TALKING.

HEY, THERE HE IS--
--MORNING, CHAMP!
WH-- WHERE AM I?
EASY BUDDY, YOU'RE IN THE HOSPITAL.
YOU'RE GONNA BE FINE.
OH GOD. FRANK, I'M SO SOR--
WHOA, HEY, STOP RIGHT THERE. YOU'VE GOT NOTHING TO APOLOGIZE FOR.
YOU JUST SAVED YOUR ASS AND MINE!
WHAT DO YOU MEAN?
YOU KIDDING? THE TABLOIDS, THEY LOVE THIS SUICIDE SHIT. AND SHOOTING YOURSELF?
IN THE CHEST?
THAT'S FUCKING HARDCORE, MAN!
BUT WHAT ABOUT THE--
OH, THIS COMPLETELY BURIED THE SEX DEVIANT STUFF. THE WHOLE THING'S JUST GIVEN YOU THIS 'DARK, EDGY, RATED-R' VIBE YOU NEVER HAD BEFORE--
--I'M TELLIN' YA, PHONE'S BEEN RINGING OFF THE HOOK WITH OFFERS ALL DAY.
YOU'RE BACK, BABY! ENJOY IT!
AND CAN I JUST SAY, ON A PERSONAL LEVEL, HOW INSPIRING IT IS TO SEE A CLIENT SHOW THIS KIND OF DEDICATION TO THEIR CAREER?
WE NEED MORE LIKE YOU, MAN. GOD BLESS YOU.
OH, AND HEY, I BROUGHT SOMEONE ALONG WITH ME, SAID THEY WANTED TO MAKE SURE YOU WERE OKAY--
--YOU RECOGNIZE HER, DON'T YOU?

IT'S THE GIRL THAT SAVED YOUR LIFE!
You have a friend request.
Sara Schmidt — 0 mutual friends
Add to list
Confirm
Ignore
Send mess
And she was.

MARLEY Z

PART 2
CONTRIBUTING TO THE DELINQUENCY OF MINORS

MARLEY ZARCONE
ART & COLORS

LETTERS
JOHNNY LOWE

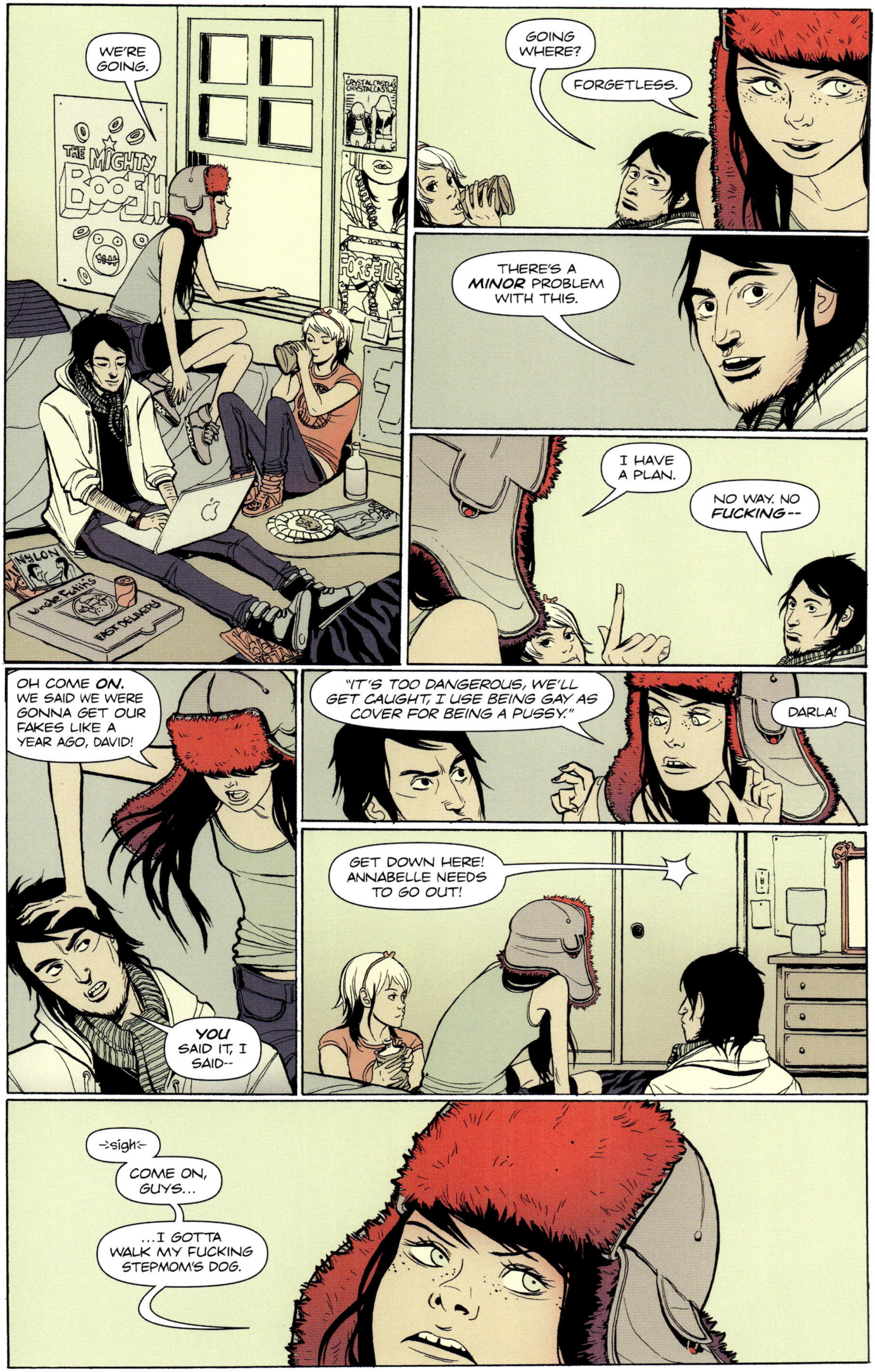
WE'RE GOING.
THE MIGHTY BOOSH
FORGETLESS
GOING WHERE?
FORGETLESS.
THERE'S A **MINOR** PROBLEM WITH THIS.
I HAVE A PLAN.
NO WAY. NO **FUCKING**--
OH COME **ON.** WE SAID WE WERE GONNA GET OUR FAKES LIKE A YEAR AGO, DAVID!
YOU SAID IT, I SAID--
"IT'S TOO DANGEROUS, WE'LL GET CAUGHT, I USE BEING GAY AS COVER FOR BEING A PUSSY."
DARLA!
GET DOWN HERE! ANNABELLE NEEDS TO GO OUT!
sigh
COME ON, GUYS...
...I GOTTA WALK MY FUCKING STEPMOM'S DOG.

LOOK, WE HAVE TO GO. WE'VE BEEN TALKING ABOUT GOING SINCE LIKE SEVENTH GRADE--
YEAH, WHEN WE TURN EIGHTEEN.
RIGHT, BUT THIS IS THE LAST ONE!
IF WE DON'T GO, THAT'S IT--
--WE'RE JUST A BUNCH OF SOUTH JERSEY ASSHOLES WHO JERKED OFF TO THEIR FLICKR, YOU KNOW?
YOU DON'T EVEN KNOW ANYONE WHO CAN GET US FAKE IDS.
PFFT!
SHOWS WHAT YOU KNOW, FRUMPSTER!
LISA RINATELLI GOT HERS FROM A GUY WORKING THE COUNTER AT THE STOP'N'GO ON STANINGTON. SAID YOU CAN GET THEM FOR TWO HUNDRED PER.
OH, GREAT PLAN--WHERE WOULD **WE** COME UP WITH TWO HUNDRED BUCKS?
EACH?
HERE.

YOU'RE THE GUY FROM CRAIG'S LIST, YOU WANTED THE CAVALIER KING CHARLES SPANIEL?
UMM... YES! YES, WHY DON'T YOU COME--
HER NAME'S ANNABELLE.
SHE PISSES A LOT.
THAT'LL BE EIGHT HUNDRED BUCKS.
TWO HUNDRED TO SPARE.
WE GOING?
BUT--
--BUT--IT'S TONIGHT!
OUR PARENTS THINK WE'RE STAYING AT YOUR PLACE, BUT YOURS--
--HOW WILL YOU...?
HEY KATHY?
HEY, IT'S ME.
ANNABELLE GOT HIT BY A TRUCK.
SORRY.
SHE'LL NEVER NOTICE I'M GONE.

SHOP 'N' GO
WHAT ARE YOU DOING? DON'T YOU NEED THE ID BEFORE YOU BUY THIS STUFF?
LISA SAID IT'S LIKE A SIGNAL.
WE GOTTA SHOW HIM THESE EXACT BOTTLES...
...WHERE THE HELL IS THE MGD?
WOW. THAT'S SOME DA VINCI CODE SHIT RIGHT THERE.
SERIOUSLY GONNA NEED TO SEE SOME ID.
Under 21 No Alcohol
We Card
A-HEM.
YEAH, SWEETHEART.
ID.
WELL...MY FRIEND LISA, SHE SAID MAYBE YOU GUYS HAVE SOME KINDA LIKE EARLY ENTRY PROGRAM FOR GIFTED YOUNGSTERS SUCH AS OURSELVES.
UH-HUH.
NICE TRY.
We Card
YOU KNOW, YOU **COULD** BE MORE RESPECTFUL OF OUR BUSINESS.
MY DAD'S BEEN BUYING HUSTLERS AT THIS STOP'N'GO FOR YEARS.

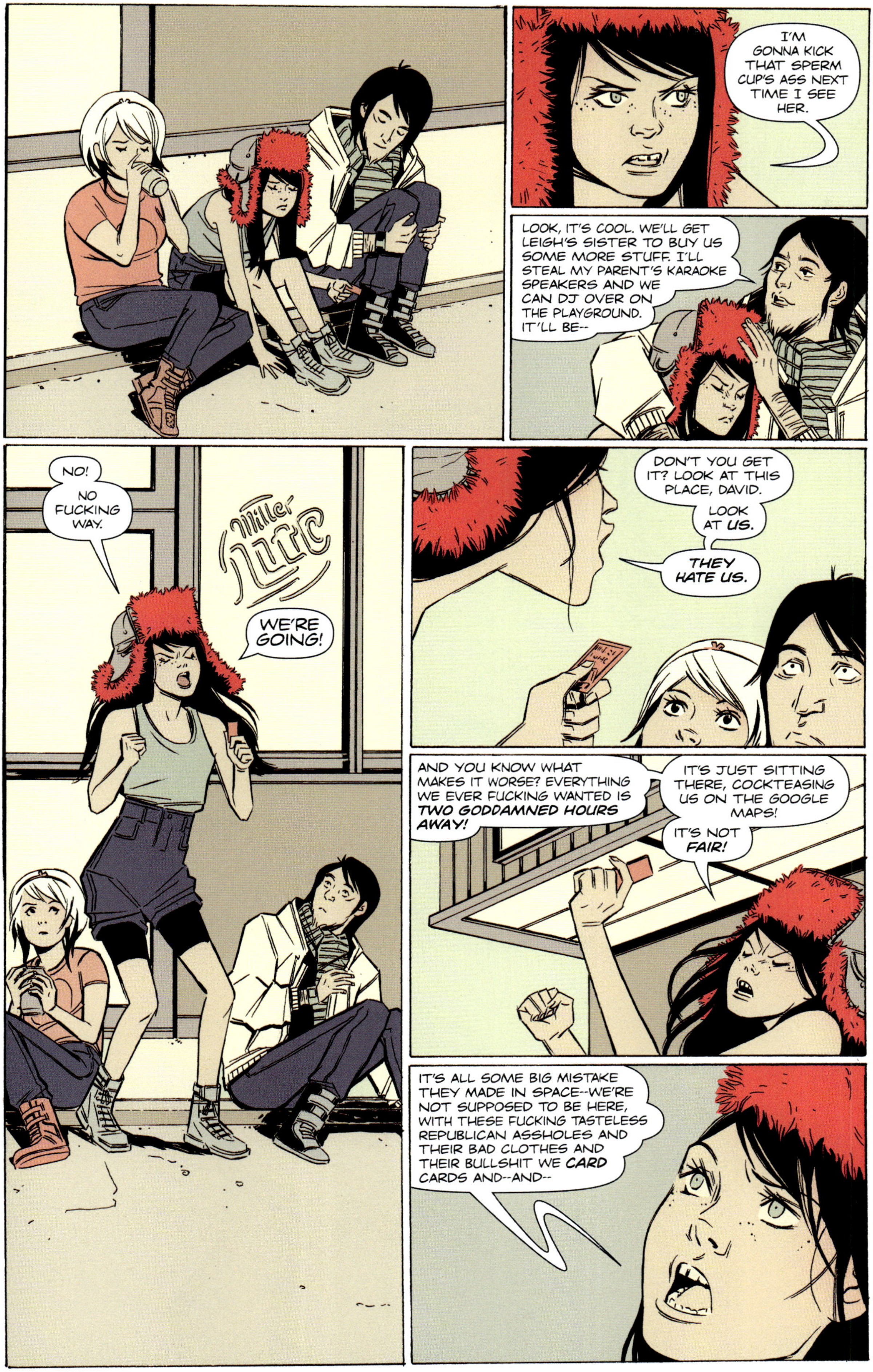
I'M GONNA KICK THAT SPERM CUP'S ASS NEXT TIME I SEE HER.
LOOK, IT'S COOL. WE'LL GET LEIGH'S SISTER TO BUY US SOME MORE STUFF. I'LL STEAL MY PARENT'S KARAOKE SPEAKERS AND WE CAN DJ OVER ON THE PLAYGROUND. IT'LL BE--
NO!
NO FUCKING WAY.
Miller Lite
WE'RE GOING!
DON'T YOU GET IT? LOOK AT THIS PLACE, DAVID.
LOOK AT **US.**
THEY HATE US.
AND YOU KNOW WHAT MAKES IT WORSE? EVERYTHING WE EVER FUCKING WANTED IS ***TWO GODDAMNED HOURS AWAY!***
IT'S JUST SITTING THERE, COCKTEASING US ON THE GOOGLE MAPS!
IT'S NOT ***FAIR!***
IT'S ALL SOME BIG MISTAKE THEY MADE IN SPACE--WE'RE NOT SUPPOSED TO BE HERE, WITH THESE FUCKING TASTELESS REPUBLICAN ASSHOLES AND THEIR BAD CLOTHES AND THEIR BULLSHIT WE **CARD** CARDS AND--AND--

WHAT-- WHAT IS IT?
IT'S AN ADDRESS.
AN ADDRESS THAT'S GONNA CHANGE OUR LIVES FOREVER.
COOL.

WELL, KNOCK ALREADY.
YOU KNOCK.
I WANT YOU TO DIE FIRST.
SIGH...YOU WERE SO HAPPY, LIKE FIVE MINUTES AGO.
THEN I REMEMBERED NOTHING GOOD EVER HAPPENS TO US.
YOU'RE GONNA MAKE SOME HAWTHORNE HEIGHTS FAN A GREAT WIFE SOMEDAY.
WELL?
UGH.
FIIIIIINE.
KNOCK KNOCK
FUCK OFF, MORMONS!
HELLO, SIR! I CAN ASSURE YOU, WE ARE NOT MORMONS! WE'RE HERE FROM THE STOP-N-GO?
ABOUT THE FALSIFIED IDENTIFICATIONS?

WHAT'D YOU GET PICKED UP FOR?
GO AWAY
UHH-- SORRY?
THE COPS.
WHAT'D THEY GET YOU FOR? I KNOW HOW THIS SHIT WORKS. I'VE BEEN DOING THIS FOR YEARS.
THEY GOT YOU FOR BEING IN THE PARK AFTER HOURS, SENT YOU TO BUST ME INSTEAD OF GOING TO A JUDGE.
I'M NOT STUPID, GOT IT?
SIR, WE OPPOSE THE FUZZ. MY FRIEND DAVID HERE RUNS A WEB SITE DEMANDING TUPAC SHAKUR'S HOMICIDE INVESTIGATION BE RE-OPENED.
WE'LL FIND THE REAL KILLERS SOMEDAY.
I GIVE YOU MY WORD, WE ARE ALL HERE OF OUR OWN RECOGNIZANCE.
WE'RE JUST THREE HARD-WORKING AND ENLIGHTENED TEENAGERS DEMANDING RIGHTS COMMENSURATE TO OUR EUROPEAN PEERS.
HRM.
ALL RIGHT, FINE, COME ON IN. BUT IF I FIND OUT YOU'RE WITH THE COPS, I'LL STAB YOU, YOU UNDERSTAND?
TAKE YOUR EYES OUT, YOU KNOW?
YOUR HOME IS LOVELY!

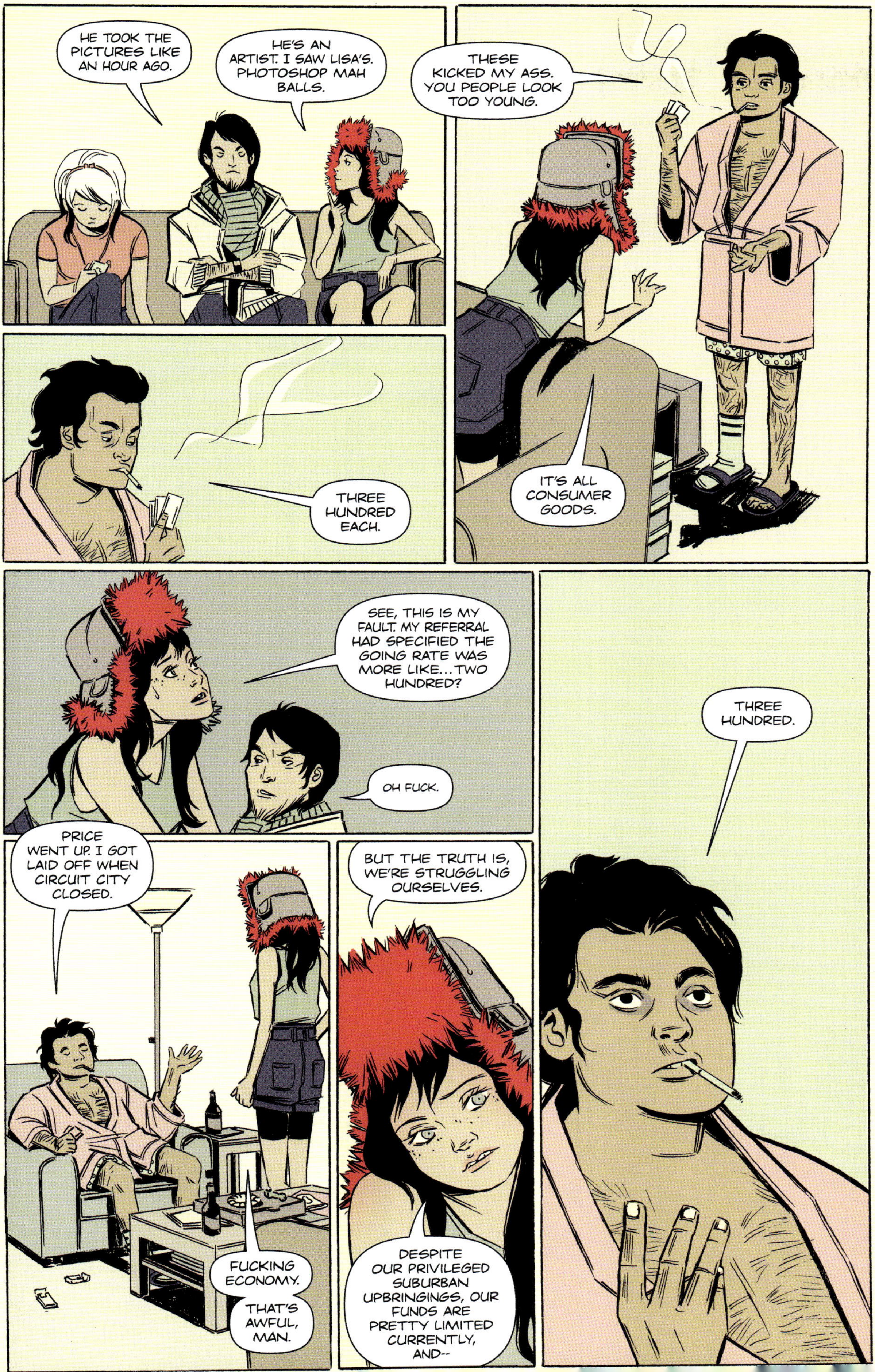
HE TOOK THE PICTURES LIKE AN HOUR AGO.
HE'S AN ARTIST. I SAW LISA'S. PHOTOSHOP MAH BALLS.
THESE KICKED MY ASS. YOU PEOPLE LOOK TOO YOUNG.
THREE HUNDRED EACH.
IT'S ALL CONSUMER GOODS.
SEE, THIS IS MY FAULT. MY REFERRAL HAD SPECIFIED THE GOING RATE WAS MORE LIKE... TWO HUNDRED?
OH FUCK.
PRICE WENT UP. I GOT LAID OFF WHEN CIRCUIT CITY CLOSED.
FUCKING ECONOMY.
THAT'S AWFUL, MAN.
BUT THE TRUTH IS, WE'RE STRUGGLING OURSELVES.
DESPITE OUR PRIVILEGED SUBURBAN UPBRINGINGS, OUR FUNDS ARE PRETTY LIMITED CURRENTLY, AND--
THREE HUNDRED.

HMMMM...WHAT IF WE THREW IN A BLOWJOB? EH, EH?
DARLA, JESUS! YOU'RE JUST GONNA WHORE YOURSELF OUT OR SOMETHING?
WHAT? NO!
NO!
I MEANT FROM YOU!
YOU BITCH--
WHAT?
YOU'RE BETTER THAN I AM.
OKAY, STRIKE THAT. NO BLOWJOB. THAT OFFER IS OFF THE TABLE FOR NOW.
FOREVER.
BUT THERE MUST BE SOMETHING WE CAN OFFER YOU TO MAKE UP THIS INSIGNIFICANT DIFFERENCE...
WHERE THE HELL ARE MY SCISSORS?

TOO BAD YOUR MOM DOESN'T HAVE ANOTHER DOG.
WAIT! I GOT IT!
OKAY, SO, BUSINESS IS SLOW, NO OTHER INCOME COMING IN RIGHT NOW, YEAH?
YEAH, THAT'S RIGHT.
AND YOU--I MEAN, YOU'RE A BUSY GUY. UNDERAGE GIRLS TO IM WITH AND ALL.
YOU'RE RUNNING AN ENTERPRISE THAT'S ALL WORD OF MOUTH, AND THAT'S GOT LIMITS.
WHAT'S YOUR POINT?
I WANNA COME WORK FOR YOU.
THIS AIN'T FUCKIN' MCDONALD'S.
HEAR ME OUT...
THIS SLEEPY LIL' TOWN'S GOT NO SHORTAGE OF UNDERAGERS TRYING TO FIND SOME WAY TO MAKE THEIR ESCAPE, AND HERE YOU ARE, WITH THE KEYS TO THE CAR. BUT EVEN TRENDSETTERS LIKE US WEREN'T MADE AWARE OF YOUR EXISTENCE 'TIL JUST RECENTLY.
YOU NEED SOMEONE ON THE STREET, SOMEONE WITH CONNECTIONS. NOT SOME ASSHOLE CLERK. SOMEONE WHO KNOWS THE KIDS AND CAN GET THE WORD OUT.
YOU NEED ME.

I CAN'T BELIEVE HE WENT FOR THAT.
DO YOU THINK I ASKED FOR A BIG ENOUGH COMMISSION?
I THOUGHT HE WOULD KILL US, AND HE ALMOST DID, BUT--
OF COURSE IT WORKED! I GOT THE ENTREPRENEURIAL SKILLS TO AVOID THE BILLS! NOW COME ON, LOSERLIES--
SURE. MAYBE SOMEDAY YOU CAN GET PROMOTED TO SELLING CRACK.
THIS TRULY IS THE LAND OF OPPORTUNITY.
WELL, I HATE TO GIVE YOU CREDIT, BUT IT WORKED.
WE GOT A TRAIN TO CATCH!

PENNSYLVANIA STATION
LOOK, I'M JUST SAYIN', WE GOTTA STOP AT GRAY'S PAPAYA FIRST. I NEED SOME BURNT PROTEIN IN THE SHAPE OF A PENIS, STAT. AND WE'RE ALREADY ON 8TH!
KISMET!
DIDN'T YOU JUST EAT LIKE A WHOLE BAG OF PEANUTS ON THE NJT?
YOU CAN'T BUILD A FOOD PYRAMID OUT OF SALT, DUDE! BESIDES, THOSE LEATHER SEATS MAKE ME SLEEPY. I NEED A PICK-ME-UP.
OKAY, FINE--BUT REMEMBER, WE NEED TO GET THERE BEFORE TEN. THEY SAY NO ONE IS GONNA GET IN AFTER TEN. NO ONE.
I PROMISE I WILL DEEP-THROAT IT. YOU JUST HAVE TO SHOW ME HOW.
HEY, WHERE'D LEIGH GO?
LEIGH--WHAT ARE YOU--?
HOLY SHIT...

OH MY GAWD--OH MY GAWD!!
IS THAT LITTLE DARLA DANBERRY?!!
I--I KNOW THAT SQUEAK.
EITHER THAT'S JENNIFER TILLY GETTING KILLED IN A CHUCKY MOVIE OR...
PAMELA VERTELLI.
WOW, IT REALLY IS YOU...
...I ALMOST DIDN'T RECOGNIZE YOU WITH YOUR DAD'S HAT ON!
NICE GLITTER.
DANS
SO WHAT BRINGS YOU TO THE BIG CITY, PUMPKIN?
YOU LIVE, LIKE, THREE BLOCKS FROM ME, PAM.

WELL, SURE, BUT SPENDING THE QUARTER AT *FIT* KEEPS ME OUTTA JERSEY MOST OF THE TIME THESE DAYS--
YOUR OUTFIT TELLS ME YOU MUST BE MISSING A LOT OF CLASSES.
THIS YOUR CORNER? 'CAUSE I'M JUST WALKING BY--
THE BF IS DRAGGING ME AND THE GIRLS OUT TO SOME PARTY TONIGHT...SOUNDS DUMB...WHAT'S THE NAME OF IT?
"FORGIVENESS?"
OH *FUCK* ME...
YOU KNOW IT?
IT'S CANCELED. THE PLACE BURNED DOWN.
A BUNCH OF GIRLS WHO LOOK ***EXACTLY LIKE YOU*** WERE TRAPPED INSIDE AND DIED, SCREAMING FOR HELP THAT NEVER CAME.
FIRE PEELED THE SKIN RIGHT OFF THEM.
OH, YOU KIDDER. SO ARE YOU GOING?
TO KILL MYSELF?
I MEAN, IS IT GOING TO BE COOL?
WHAT, KILLING MYSELF? IN COMPARISON TO THIS, YES.
HA HA, YOU'RE SO FUNNY, SWEETIE.
WELL, I GOTTA SCRAM--WE'RE HITTING *TICK TOCK* FOR A BITE...
I GUESS WE'LL SEE YOU THERE, FRECKLEFACE!

I KNOW WHAT YOU'RE GOING TO SAY, BUT--
WE'RE GOING HOME.
DARLA--
I'M SERIOUS. THIS IS A SIGN.
I SHOULD POINT OUT, YOU AND HER USED TO BE BEST FRIENDS.
YEAH, AND THEN SHE STOLE JASON FENWICK AWAY FROM ME JUST BECAUSE SHE WAS READY FOR HANDJOBS!
IT WAS SEVENTH GRADE, DEAR.
YEAH, WELL, I GUESS ALL THAT FOOLING AROUND WITH HER UNCLE FINALLY PAID OFF FOR HER THERE.
AND NOW SHE GOES AND TAKES THE FIT QUARTER AWAY FROM ME!
I CAN'T BELIEVE I USED TO SHARE A CUCUMBER WITH THAT GIRL.
NOW, DARLA, SHE WON THAT, FAIR AND--
CORSAGES, DAVID!
SHE WON BY DESIGNING FUCKING CORSAGES! WHO THE HELL GOES TO FIT SO THEY CAN WORK IN PROM RENTALS?!!
I DESERVED IT. MY STUFF WAS--
YOUR STUFF WAS WARHOL. YOU KNOW IT WAS.
WHICH IS WHY, WHEN WE GRADUATE, WE ARE GONNA COME UP HERE, AND START OUR OWN NIGHT, AND YOU ARE GONNA DESIGN--

NO, WE'RE NOT! DON'T YOU GET IT?
WE'RE TOO LATE! LIKE, TEN YEARS TOO LATE!
THIS IS **HER** PLACE NOW.
I MEAN, HOW THE FUCK IS A GIRL LIKE PAMPON GETTING INTO FORGETLESS?
BECAUSE THIS WHOLE GODDAMNED CITY'S BEEN OVERRUN BY THE SAME PEOPLE WE'RE TRYING TO GET AWAY FROM, THAT'S WHY!
PEOPLE LIKE US, WE'LL BE LIVING IN BROOKLYN AND PRETENDING TO LIKE WILLIAMSBURG. YOU CAN TRY TO GROW MORE FACIAL HAIR, WE CAN ACT BORED IN BARS WITH DEER HEADS ON THE WALL.
FACE IT, THE WHOLE PLACE IS OVER. NEW YORK DOESN'T EXIST ANYMORE. AND BY THE TIME IT DOES AGAIN, I'LL BE FAT AND MARRIED AND YOU'LL BE DEAD FROM THE **AIDS.**
WE'VE BEEN DREAMING ABOUT THIS SINCE OUR FIRST PERIODS, BUT THAT'S ALL IT IS, A BIG, DUMB DREAM.
WHAT DO YOU WANT ME TO SAY? YOU'RE GONNA LET ONE RUN-IN WITH THAT SKANK RUIN YOUR NIGHT? RUIN **NEW YORK?**
IT'S THAT EASY TO TAKE DOWN THE GREAT DARLA DANBERRY?
LOOK, EVEN IF IT DOES SUCK, EVEN IF EVERYTHING SUCKS, AT LEAST WE DO IT TOGETHER. AT LEAST YOU CAN MAKE FUN OF IT ALL WITH ME AND LE--
--GREAT.
NOW WHERE'D SHE GO?

PAPAYA
OPEN 24
sigh
C'MON, THEN...
...WE GOTTA GET THERE BEFORE TEN.

9:45
remember the UTAH SAINTS
9:51
FEED KIDS
9:56
9:59
I DON'T BELIEVE THIS...
10:00

PLEASE TELL ME YOU ARE IN LINE FOR SOME KIND OF KINGS OF LEON BULLSHIT.
DON'T EVEN LOOK AT MY SPOT, BITCH.
I FEEL AT HOME ALREADY!
YOU REALIZE THERE'S NO WAY WE'RE GETTING IN, RIGHT?
THIS LINE IS FOR THE SHOW. IT'S WHERE THEY PUT THE...
...OH MY GOD.
IT'S WHERE THEY PUT THE PEOPLE FROM NEW JERSEY.
YOU KNOW, IT'S LIKE WE NEVER WATCHED THE JOURNEY OF NATTY GANN TOGETHER. PERSEVERANCE, DUDE! I HAVE A PLAN!
FOR THE LAST TIME, I AM NOT GIVING ANYONE A BLOWJOB.
OKAY, WELL... I'LL COME UP WITH SOMETHING ELSE THEN.

I'M THINKING, DECEMBERIST.
10:51
YOU SURE PICKED A SHIT TIME TO STOP BEING CREATIVE.
11:47
DAMMIT.
1:07
THESE PEOPLE ARE IMPERVIOUS TO MY CLEVERNESS.
WELL, THEN I FEEL AT HOME ALREADY.
I GOT IT.
WE CAN WAIT THEM OUT. 3 A.M. COMES AROUND, THEY'LL ALL GIVE UP. AND WE'LL BE WAITING.
2:15
THAT'S IT? THAT'S WHAT YOU GOT? WAIT THEM OUT?
I'M TELLING YOU, IT'S GONNA WORK.
2:41
THIS LINE IS NOTHING BUT PUSSIES.
DARLA, HEY WAKE UP--WE--WE'RE NEXT!
NO FUCKIN' WAY--
3:00

UH-UH.
WAIT, WHAT DO YOU MEAN, NO? WE--
AS IN NO.
AS IN, YOU WILL NEVER BE THERE, YOU WILL BE ONLY HERE, SWEETIE-PIE.
WHAT THE FUCK ARE YOU TALKING ABOUT?!!
WE HAVE TO GET IN THERE, DO YOU UNDERSTAND?!!
WE BELONG IN THERE!!!
LISTEN TO ME--
NO, NO, YOU LISTEN HERE, JUNO. I BEEN WORKING THIS LINE FOR SIX YEARS, HONEY. AND IN THOSE SIX YEARS, YOU KNOW HOW MANY POST-PUBESCENT BRIDGE AND TUNNEL HOODRATS I'VE LET IN THE DOOR WITH THOSE CHEAP-ASS FAKE IDS?
THAT'S RIGHT, YOU ALREADY KNOW.
AND THAT NUMBER, SWEETIE-- IS NOT GOING FROM ZERO TO THREE.
SO I WANT YOU TO TAKE BRIGHT EYES AND SILENT BONITA HERE, AND WHATEVER'S LEFT ON YOUR URBAN OUTFITTERS GIFT CARD, AND GET THE FUCK OUT OF MY LINE.

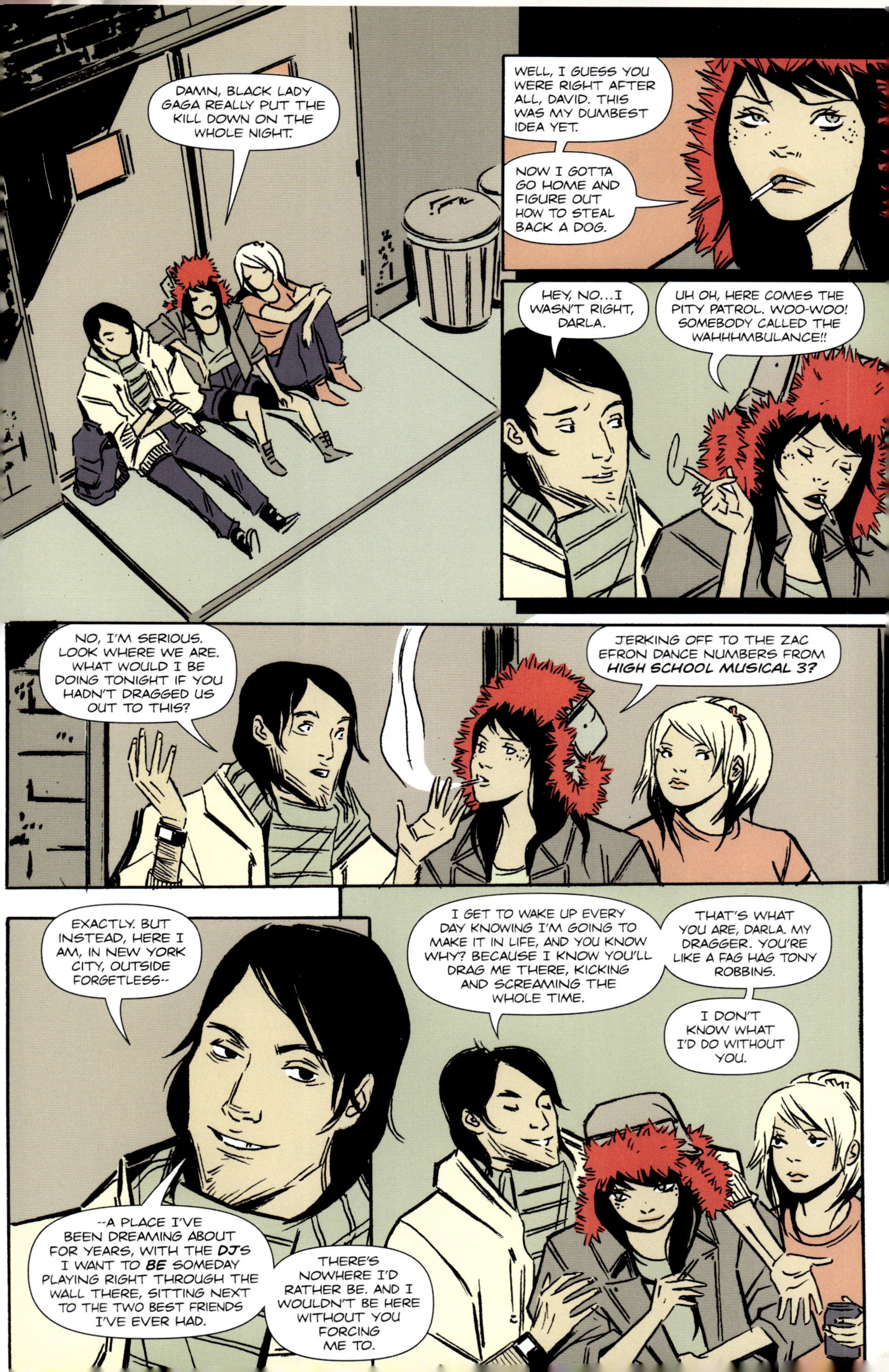
DAMN, BLACK LADY GAGA REALLY PUT THE KILL DOWN ON THE WHOLE NIGHT.
WELL, I GUESS YOU WERE RIGHT AFTER ALL, DAVID. THIS WAS MY DUMBEST IDEA YET.
NOW I GOTTA GO HOME AND FIGURE OUT HOW TO STEAL BACK A DOG.
HEY, NO... I WASN'T RIGHT, DARLA.
UH OH, HERE COMES THE PITY PATROL. WOO-WOO! SOMEBODY CALLED THE WAHHHMBULANCE!!
NO, I'M SERIOUS. LOOK WHERE WE ARE. WHAT WOULD I BE DOING TONIGHT IF YOU HADN'T DRAGGED US OUT TO THIS?
JERKING OFF TO THE ZAC EFRON DANCE NUMBERS FROM HIGH SCHOOL MUSICAL 3?
EXACTLY. BUT INSTEAD, HERE I AM, IN NEW YORK CITY, OUTSIDE FORGETLESS--
--A PLACE I'VE BEEN DREAMING ABOUT FOR YEARS, WITH THE DJS I WANT TO BE SOMEDAY PLAYING RIGHT THROUGH THE WALL THERE, SITTING NEXT TO THE TWO BEST FRIENDS I'VE EVER HAD.
THERE'S NOWHERE I'D RATHER BE. AND I WOULDN'T BE HERE WITHOUT YOU FORCING ME TO.
I GET TO WAKE UP EVERY DAY KNOWING I'M GOING TO MAKE IT IN LIFE, AND YOU KNOW WHY? BECAUSE I KNOW YOU'LL DRAG ME THERE, KICKING AND SCREAMING THE WHOLE TIME.
THAT'S WHAT YOU ARE, DARLA. MY DRAGGER. YOU'RE LIKE A FAG HAG TONY ROBBINS.
I DON'T KNOW WHAT I'D DO WITHOUT YOU.

AWWW...THAT'S THE NICEST THING ANYONE'S EVER SAID TO ME!
SWEET.
SO WHAT DO WE DO NOW?
ARE YOU KIDDING?
WE'RE GONNA SIT OUT HERE, LISTEN TO THE SETLIST--
--AND TWITTER-PRETEND WE'RE INSIDE SO THAT EVERYONE BACK HOME GETS JEALOUS.
YEAH, WOULDA BEEN NICE TO GET IN THOUGH, RIGHT? I CAN'T BELIEVE THAT TRANSJEALOUS BITCH RUINED IT FOR US!
AFTER ALL WE WENT THROUGH TO GET HERE.
AND NOW WE GOTTA SIT OUT HERE LIKE THE HOMELESS RUNAWAYS WE LACK THE NERVE TO BE AND--
--OW, WATCH IT, NICO!
IT CANNOT-- IT CANNOT BE THAT EASY.
CANNOT IT?

DAAAAAAAVID!!! I NEED A DRAAAAAAAANK!! FOR MAH MOOOOOUTH!!!
HUH? NO, HEY, GET LEIGH TO GET IT.
SHE'S BUSY!
BUSY WITH WHAT? WHERE IS SHE, ANYWAY?
FUCK.

TWO GIN AND TONICS, PLEASE.
LITTLE YOUNG FOR THAT AREN'T YOU, SWEETIE?
OH MY GOD.
RELAX. I WAS LIKE SIXTEEN WHEN WE GOT STARTED HERE.
YOU'RE ERIC FREDRICKSONN! I MEAN--YOU'RE THE DJ!
HE'S THE RAPPER.
I'M SORRY, IT'S JUST...I AM **SERIOUSLY** A FAN. REALLY.
NOT LIKE THESE PEOPLE.
THIS IS YOUR FIRST TIME HERE, ISN'T IT?
YEAH.
I MEAN, ME AND MY FRIENDS DARLA AND LEIGH, WE, UH--WELL, YOU PROBABLY DON'T WANNA HEAR IT, BUT...WE WENT THROUGH A **LOT** TO GET HERE.
WORTH IT?

JESUS, YES. YOU HAVE NO IDEA HOW LONG WE'VE BEEN FANS.
I MEAN, I LEARNED HOW TO DJ LISTENING TO YOU AND TRAVIS' MIXES.
YOU'RE A DJ?
ME AND DARLA, YEAH. WE DO PLAYGROUNDS, MOSTLY.
YOU WANNA DO IT HERE?
DO WHAT? HAVE SEX WITH YOU?
DJ, IDIOT.
HUH?
LOOK, TRAVIS ALREADY WENT HOME WITH SOME BERLIN SKANK. ANNIE'S COKED OUT OF HER MIND. I'M GONNA BE THE ONLY ONE UP THERE, AND I'M ALREADY BORED OUT OF MY MIND.
I'M ABOUT TO PLAY *DELOREAN*, AND I HAVE NO IDEA HOW TO TOP IT. YOU WANNA TAKE OVER?
BUT--IT'S YOUR LAST NIGHT!
LAST NIGHT OF ***WHAT?!!*** WE'VE GOT GIGS IN PARIS AND MILAN NEXT MONTH. NEW YORK IS OVER, AT LEAST FOR US IT IS.
I FEEL LIKE PASSING THE TORCH.
JUST DON'T CUM ON MY MACBOOK.
YOU IN?
YES! FUCK ***YES!*** JUST--JUST LET ME FIND--
GO GET HER.

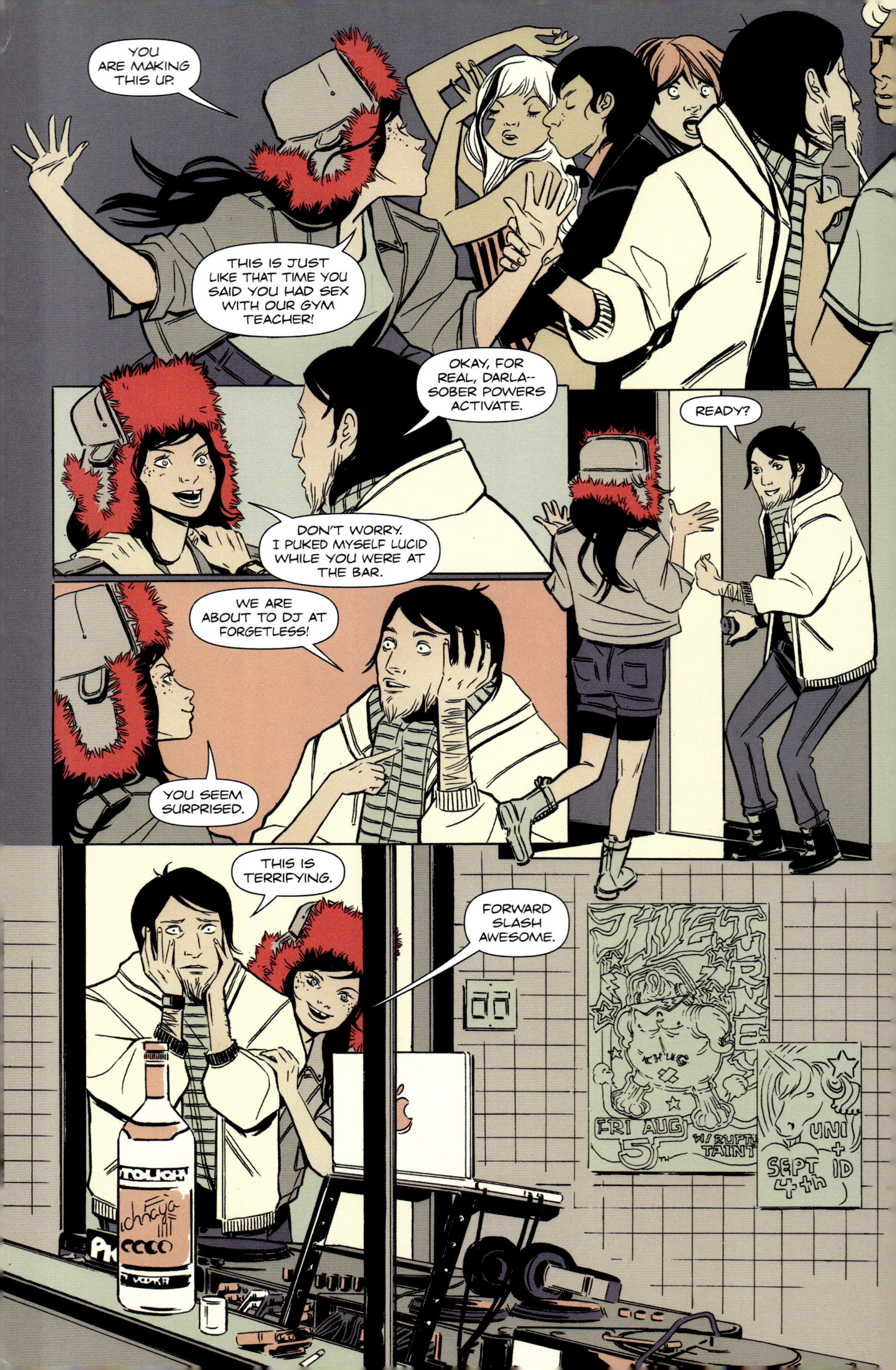
YOU ARE MAKING THIS UP.
THIS IS JUST LIKE THAT TIME YOU SAID YOU HAD SEX WITH OUR GYM TEACHER!
OKAY, FOR REAL, DARLA-- SOBER POWERS ACTIVATE.
DON'T WORRY. I PUKED MYSELF LUCID WHILE YOU WERE AT THE BAR.
WE ARE ABOUT TO DJ AT FORGETLESS!
YOU SEEM SURPRISED.
READY?
THIS IS TERRIFYING.
FORWARD SLASH AWESOME.
FRI AUG 5th
UNI + ID
SEPT 4th
VODKA

LOOK DAVID, WE DO THIS... IT CAN'T JUST BE ONE AND DONE, YOU KNOW?
I KNOW WE WERE SUPPOSED TO WAIT A COUPLE YEARS AND SAVE UP AND MOVE, THEN WE'D START A NIGHT SOMEWHERE--
BUT THIS IS LIKE A ONCE-IN-A-WASTED LIFETIME OPPOR--
DARLA, STOP.
JUST LET ME--
I SAID STOP.
YOU DON'T HAVE TO GIVE ME A BIG SPEECH THIS TIME.
I'M WITH YOU. ALL THE WAY.
I LOVE YOU, STEREOTYPICAL GAY BEST FRIEND.
...WE'RE RUNNING AWAY FROM HOME, AREN'T WE?
RELAX--
--WE'LL ALWAYS GO BACK FOR CHRISTMAS.

TITLE
BAPTISM
NEW IN TOWN
IDEALISIC
CRYSTAL CASTLES
LITTLE BOOTS
DIGITALISM
R.I.P.
HERE LIES
FORGETLESS
2004 - 2009
LONG LIVE
NO ID
2009 - ???

Coverless?__01

W. Scott Forbes - Art & Colors

Uploaded October 12, 2010
by ellelauryn

– ellelauryn's photostream

5
uploads

browse

Tags

- Extra Features
- Cover Gallery
- W. Scott Forbes
- Marley Zarcone
- Forgetless Series Artists

Additional Information

Anyone can see this photo

- Taken with a Kodak P880 Zoom.
- More properties
- Taken on May 22, 2009

Viewed 21 times

Would you like to comment?

Sign up for a free account, or sign in (if you're already a member).

Coverless?__02_03

Marley Zarcone - Art & Colors

W. Scott Forbes - Art & Colors

Uploaded October 12, 2010
by ellelauryn

– ellelauryn's photostream

5
uploads

browse

Tags

- Extra Features
- Cover Gallery
- W. Scott Forbes
- Marley Zarcone
- Forgetless Series Artists

Additional Information

- Anyone can see this photo
- Taken with a Kodak P880 Zoom.
- More properties
- Taken on May 22, 2009
- Viewed 21 times

Would you like to comment?

Sign up for a free account, or sign in (if you're already a member).

Coverless?__04_05

Marley Zarcone - Art & Colors

W. Scott Forbes - Art & Colors

Uploaded October 12, 2010
by ellelauryn

– ellelauryn's photostream

browse

5
uploads

Tags

- Extra Features
- Cover Gallery
- W. Scott Forbes
- Marley Zarcone
- Forgetless Series Artists

Additional Information

Anyone can see this photo

- Taken with a Kodak P880 Zoom.
- More properties
- Taken on May 22, 2009

Viewed 21 times

Would you like to comment?

Sign up for a free account, or sign in (if you're already a member).